THE UNNATURAL HISTORY OF CYPRESS PARISH

ALSO BY ELISE BLACKWELL

Hunger

THE UNNATURAL HISTORY OF CYPRESS PARISH

ELISE BLACKWELL

UNBRIDLED
BOOKS

This is a work of fiction. The names, characters, places and incidents are either the product of the author's imagination or are used fictitiously, and any resemblance to actual persons living or dead, business establishments, events, or locales is entirely coincidental.

Unbridled Books
Denver, Colorado

Library of Congress Cataloging-in-Publication Data

Blackwell, Elise
The unnatural history of Cypress Parish / Elise Blackwell.
p. cm.
ISBN 13: 978-1-932961-31-7 (ALK. PAPER)
ISBN-10: 1-932961-31-3 (ALK. PAPER)
1. Reminiscing in old age—Fiction. 2. New Orleans (La.)—Fiction.
I. Title.
PS3602.L3257U56 2007
813'.6—DC22 2007000106

3 5 7 9 10 8 6 4 2

Book Design by SH • CV

Second Printing

In memory of my grandparents:

Robert Elliott May Sr.
Renee Elise David May
Will Hoyle Blackwell Sr.
Lois Fredonia Taylor Blackwell

"They call it regional, this relevance—
the deepest place we have: in this pool forms
the model of our land, a lonely one,
responsive to the wind. Everything we own
has brought us here: from here we speak."

—William Stafford, from "Lake Chelan"

"We shall pick up an existence by its frogs."

—Charles Fort, from *Lo!*

THE UNNATURAL HISTORY OF CYPRESS PARISH

PROLOGUE

am a man far removed from his origins—by miles, by years, and by more intangible measures. Every piece of wood, no matter how refined and sanded, is marked by the conditions where the tree was grown. The mix of nutrients in the soil and air, the shifts in temperature and humidity, high winds and lightning, the damage from insects and wood-boring birds, and cultivation—the human history of the land—leave their evidence. Who I am remains intimately gnarled with where I came from. And where I came from is the place making the news, the place in the line of fire, soon to be the eye of the storm. Though I've pruned from my speech all traces of accent, I'm from south of south. I am from Cypress Parish, Louisiana.

These days, Cypress Parish isn't so very different from other places. The small towns of Cypress Parish angle in odd triangles, pointing from the highway that now clears a straight line to New Orleans. Defying swamp, people live in groups of brick houses laid out in flat grids in the 1960s or in newer houses with high ceilings and bigger windows and thinner walls, pocking roads that curve artificially around man-made hills and ponds claimed and quartered from marsh.

Most of the parish's citizens drive to work in New Orleans or in the state capital, where men and a few women sign good laws as well as the statutes that give Louisiana its turn—with one or two other states—as national laughingstock. A few commute to the other nearby city, which is really only a large town and which crossed the national radar screen just once, when a spree murderer killed seven people in one of its casinos.

The people now boarding their windows in Cypress shop in the strip malls and club stores that most of the parish towns now boast. Those who are not Catholic worship in the large, well-advertised churches that the South has exported to the rest of the country. Like people in the rest of the country, they eat breakfast cereals out of colorful boxes and watch cable television. They attend their children's games and plays and school carnivals. They go to work willingly in the morning but are glad to come home in the evening.

If a man driving through the parish on his way to somewhere else took one of the exit ramps leading from the highway, stopping off for the weak coffee and clean restrooms that make fast-food restaurants a traveler's oasis, he would see the worst of what our country offers with none of its best. Though he might catch a clean whiff of pine when the breeze blows in from the east or of the salty Gulf when the wind moves south to north, he'd be as likely to breathe a noseful of the stink that only a paper mill can churn out. Nothing that entered his field of vision would strike him as reason to linger. He would, more than likely, finish the paper cup of whatever it was he sought refreshment in, seal himself back in his air-conditioned car, and be glad of the easy funnel back onto the highway.

But if for any reason he found himself driving the smaller roads that link the parish towns without reference to the no-nonsense stretch of clean black asphalt, his eyes would light on more peculiar things. If he was attentive, he'd pick up everywhere remnants of life as it used to be lived, of life as it was lived there and not quite the same way as anywhere else.

If he followed the winding two-lane road between Cypress, the town where I was reared, and Banville, the closest French town, he might identify a few stands of trees with the exact mix of cypress, oak, and pine that could be found before the logging companies bought, used, and then left this land. If he got out to relieve his traveler's bladder behind one of those trees, he might be startled by one of the spotted salamanders that have lived there since before people and that live nowhere else in the world.

If he had call to go on to Banville or was driven there by some back-road curiosity he couldn't quite name and found himself in the town with no excuse, he might notice that the finely made Catholic church, with its jewel-colored windows that seem to melt in the afternoon heat, still looks out of place. It sits as a clumsy testament to some long-removed Old World grandeur in a town where the wealthiest man is a hardworking lawyer and people are, more or less, still poor.

And if he entered Banville's oyster bar—not the new one up by the highway but the one just off the town square, where the oysters are the freshest but the dirty concrete floors frighten away even those tourists seeking what they call *the authentic*—he would hear the flat local French still spoken with both emphasis and speed by the men who shuck the mollusks.

Chain restaurants are as trusted in the town of Cypress as they are everywhere, but a traveler can still find places, if he heads just south of the bedroom communities, where biscuits are made from scratch every morning, using fresh buttermilk and cut with an old water glass, places where the ham served spent weeks in a tilted, hand-built smoke shed and came from an animal that, for its allotted time, had a name.

If he pressed farther south, against the Gulf breeze that is sometimes mild but now blows with the force of the coming hurricane, he would hear more of the French patois but also a Spanish laced with its Canary Island origins though cut off from those roots for more than two centuries. In one village, he would hear more Italian than any other language spoken. If one of the women there caught him admiring her lush vegetable garden, she might invite him in for a flute of carbonated wine made from her homegrown oranges, and he would understand that the invitation was an order, that he could not say no to her.

Indeed there are sundry reminders of what life was like before my father and men like him and some unlike him laid rail and felled trees and, through their labor and sometimes treachery, made the soft, sterile bed on which we rest our modern lives. For anyone who listens closely and looks with attention, there are suggestions everywhere of life as it was lived before men with the power of money changed it forever.

And if a traveler were to come across an establishment more or less untouched by our national fads and fetishes, if he entered and waited patiently over a cup of strong coffee for the best shrimp stew he could ever hope to eat, if he eavesdropped on the old-timers—usually claiming stools at the counter and smoking cigarettes if they still can—he should not be surprised, not even a little, when one of their stories is about the water that rose in 1927. And he should not be surprised, not even a little, when one of those stories is about my father, William Proby, or about Olivier Menard or one of the other men whose names, before the flood, mattered.

Here on the eve of what the newscasters say will be more devastation by water, it is a few of these stories that I try to tell, mixing as best I can what I saw with my own eyes and what I understood later to be fact into the most complete picture I am capable of making. Yet the older I get, and despite all my training as a man of reason and method, the harder I find it to understand anything at all. If you were to place, side by side, the historical account of something that happened, a painting of it, and a scientific explanation of how and why it occurred, you might still not understand it unless, maybe, you lived through it yourself. Even then, you'd succumb to forgetting. An old man may remember the facts of his youth, but he cannot always remember what they felt like.

PART ONE

BACKWATER

he strange and wet spring I turned seventeen and crossed the marshy border that separates all that is good and bad of boyhood from all that is good and bad of manhood, three men tried to kill my father. Then water and the actions of men washed away almost everything I knew.

The first incident rose like steam from nowhere but the damp ground and was over before it had time to worry anyone other than me.

My father, William Proby, had worked in logging since he was thirteen years old, when the lumber company showed up with a dollar for any young man willing to lay track and fell the backwoods he'd crawled out of. My father had started as a water boy and then, through brains and sweat labor and some said cunning if not treachery, moved into skilled positions. He'd thought and muscled his way from locomotive engineer to loader operator to drum puller to skidder foreman to camp foreman. Then, a scant few years before the spring in which three men sought to halt his rise, he was made superintendent of the town of Cypress.

Though he could not have known it would be Cypress—and indeed Cypress had not existed on the map or anywhere else before the lumber company thought it up and made it a place—becoming company-town superintendent had been my father's plan since he was that thirteen-year-old water boy.

There were men in Cypress with more education, men who'd matriculated in social strata that my father would never touch: the town's doctor and dentist, of course, and even Gaspar Anderson, the painter who roomed parts of the year with the Washburn women. But no one in town ranked higher than my father. No one was over him, not since he had taken care of the constable. Charles Segrist didn't really count. Everyone knew that, as company representative, Mr. Segrist limited his Cypress rounds to a few days a week, preferring to spend most of his time in New Orleans, where, as he put it, his true interests lay.

One Saturday early in the new year, I was riding the rails with my father on a gas-motored cart adapted to stay on the tracks by the addition of flanges to the inner walls of its four wheels. From a distance, my father was still larger than life to me, but, sitting side by side, I could remember that I had already grown taller than his six feet even, though he could still take me in boxing, arm wrestling, and nearly every other physical feat save running. Aging had taken more than a little of his speed.

Anyone could see, though, even when he was seated, that

my father was strong. He was a man to decide things quickly, a man to reckon with. His feet were always right under him, his body forward, his head at the very top of his neck, ready to strike.

We were riding the rails, checking in on the Negro crews. The last stop of the morning was Rabbit's crew, which was digging ditch for a skidder line on a new plot.

Rabbit and my father had become something akin to friends during our first week in Cypress. The town constable, a blunt-looking man known to be slow to move but quick to temper, had quarreled with Rabbit over the constable's efforts to arrest Rabbit's brother Ernest for selling gin in the tunk he ran down in the Negro quarter.

My father ordinarily took a dim view of bootlegging, a view that only darkened after my Uncle Walter was killed by a man who ran liquor from the coast up to New Orleans. But his attitude was somewhat softer concerning liquor and black men, who, he said, could more understandably take to drink because they had nothing to work toward, no way to rise without leaving their home, not even through brains and sweat labor.

Rabbit and the constable—some said just Rabbit and others said only the constable—had exchanged shots in the street, right down from the Washburn women's boardinghouse. Rabbit had run into the woods south of town, where the constable had been afraid to chase him, he'd said, given that the woods ran right alongside the Negro quarter. "You know how people stick beside their own kind," he'd said by way of explanation.

Upon hearing the constable's version, my father had gone in

after Rabbit himself. The two had come back to town in under an hour, Rabbit agreeing to be locked in the jail. Within a few days, though, my father had convinced the lumber company that Cypress had little or more likely no need for a superintendent and a constable both. And once the constable was out of the picture and soon enough out of town, my father released Rabbit and placed him on the crew he now oversaw. My father told my mother that he didn't know if he was madder at the constable for being scared of the woods or for escalating a situation that should have been kept small. "Man's an idiot," he'd said and shook his head while he was smiling.

I never found out what my father had said to Rabbit in the woods. I'd wanted to ask at the time and for a long while afterward, but I understood that my father was the sort of man who told you what he wanted you to know and didn't appreciate any questions that went beyond that.

We maneuvered the gasoline-powered cart in fairly close to where the crew was digging before climbing down and continuing on foot. The morning chill had evaporated, leaving a day that was unusually hot for late winter. Shade was better than no shade, but even in the curved world made by the wood's canopy, the air felt like warm, damp wool. It was loud with insects low to the ground and with the birds overhead.

Rabbit approached with steps that took him as much side to side as forward due to his short, bowed legs. But he was a big man on top of them, with a round chest and an unusually large head. I didn't know why he was called Rabbit, but I knew it had nothing to do with how he looked or moved.

"One of the men was just carrying on," Rabbit started up, "in some detail about how when he married his wife, she could pee through the eye of a needle but now she can't even hit a wash bucket without splashing."

While my father laughed, Rabbit shot me an eye. "But perhaps I shouldn't be repeating such tales in front of your boy," he said. "A fine boy, too, taller every day from the looks of things. What you going to make out of him, Mr. Proby?"

My father nodded with something that struck me as closer to ordinary satisfaction than any real pride and gave the answer he always gave: "Louis will be a doctor."

"I'll be learning anatomy," I said, "and from the sound of your man's story, he could use to study some too."

Though my delivery was stiff—I wasn't used to talking with grown men and certainly unaccustomed to offering humor—my father and Rabbit appeared to find my comment funny enough. Both laughed hard, Rabbit even rubbing the side of his sizable belly. But Rabbit stopped his laugh in the middle of his throat, dampening it to a low growl and then cutting it off altogether. He moved closer, almost into us, and whispered to my father that one of the men, the one with the blue bandana hanging from his jumper, had brought a gun on the job and bragged that he was going to use it on the superintendent.

My father smiled and nodded, as though he had just been told another connubial joke. Then he cracked all the knuckles of his right hand, working one finger at a time, base to tip, and started over toward the men.

I moved to follow, but Rabbit pressed a large palm flat against my chest. The dampness of his hand soaked into my shirt, its warmth spreading like a stain. I could smell his sweat, more bitter than sharp, like the rind rather than the flesh of a lemon.

Rabbit shook his head, almost with just his eyes. "Your father knows what to do. Let him handle his business."

The large man let me edge a few inches to one side so that I could see around him, but he stayed close, his hand ready to stall me again. And then he asked me question after question about my mother, sisters, and my little brother, whose name was Powell but whom everyone called Pal.

I murmured the answers with all the politeness I could muster but without much concentration. "Just fine," I said. "Yes, Luta's still crazy for basketball, playing it or watching it, but especially playing it." "Emily sure is as pretty as ever and, yes, sweet as sugar, too." "No, he still won't dress his own game, says his stomach won't take it."

As I muttered my responses in turn with Rabbit's questions, I watched and listened to my father make his way down the line of working men. He paused before each, commenting on the fine work of one, the marriage of another's daughter, the well-being of the next man's wife or fiancée.

"If you ask me," said Rabbit, "a boy's old enough to hunt, a boy's old enough to skin."

I had to look directly at him then and laugh, because that was the same thought I'd been keeping to myself for a good year or more. "I'll agree with you there," I said.

When I put my eyes back to my father, he was standing right in front of the man with the blue bandana, just one step up the ditch grade, making a remark about the shovel the man was using, asking to see it, looking with concern at its handle as he took it from the man's hands.

Then, cottonmouth fast, he swung full force and hit the man across the side of his face with the flat of the shovel. The man did not raise a hand, nor did he duck or reel back. He dropped straight, face down in the ditch water. A spotted salamander skittered away as my father reached under the injured man's jumper, swiftly removed the revolver as though he'd known just where it was hidden, and tucked it under his own shirt. None of the men reacted.

Rabbit stopped interviewing me then, and together we watched my father continue down the line, spending a particularly long time congratulating one older man on the acceptance of his grandson into a Negro divinity school up north.

Before he walked over to pull the fallen man's face from the brackish water, Rabbit smiled at me and said, "I told you he knew what to do."

My father did not pay the would-be assailant another look on his way back to the cart. As we followed the tracks home through stands of hardwood and then pine, all he said was, "Don't mention any of that business to your mother."

My early training in science would, as you'd expect, include lectures on the importance of scientific method, of developing and testing hypotheses, of experiment as the crucial successor to observation if not sometimes its antecedent.

Yet I have kept into my deep old age—at first in a desk drawer, later in a thoughtless cardboard box on the shelf of a seldom-used closet, and now on the corner of the work desk made from a single cypress plank—my notebooks on the natural history of Cypress Parish, begun the year before the great flood.

During spans of my life, I have gone a decade or more without leafing through them. At other ages, I read through most of the entries at least every year or two, laughing at my youthful attempts at accuracy through thoroughness, as though quantity could substitute for wisdom, an avalanche of fact and physical description for the profundity of the single telling detail, every aspect of a thing's appearance for its essence.

My entry on the armadillo dwelled, for three paragraphs, on the animal's hoof-like footprints. It mentions that the front foot is four-toed but fails to describe its awkward delicacy in contrast to the more plodding five-toed back foot. I troubled myself to mention, perhaps because at the time I thought the observation original, that the insect-eater was the only local animal to dishevel ant hills. I didn't mention, because I didn't yet know, that the armadillo is the culprit behind the tenacious prevalence of leprosy in Louisiana and eastern Texas.

More egregious, the entry mentioned the animal's peculiar shell only in passing and failed to suggest its function—protection—at all. I missed the point. Perhaps the whole project had missed the point. The flood would hide the natural world only by water. Over months, that water would be sucked into the earth or spill back into the river that had carried it or roll over the plane of sunken earth to add harmlessly to the volume of the Gulf of Mexico. Some of the species of tree and amphibian and moss and bayou snake that I labored to describe are today endangered. But even today, no plant or animal named in my notebooks belongs only to the past.

It is the other world, with its precise and unrepeatable configuration of human relationships and man-made things, that I pain myself to remember because I failed to record it, even to myself, as significant. It is the human world that was proved ephemeral by the shimmering sea that had been land.

We were still living in a yellow-brown house on block ten of Cypress's numbered grid of streets. Majestic Mustard was what the paint can named the color. It was the finest house we had ever lived in, but we were poised to move into one even bigger and better.

From the year I was born until the day we moved to Cypress, my family lived in logging camps. Most of the time, we lived in one cabin or another, though for a stretch we lived in a converted passenger car parked on a side track. After my father made camp superintendent, we most often managed to get two cabins, which my father set twelve or so feet apart and connected with scrap lumber into a three-room house, one room a kitchen to which my father would attach a small porch for washing. Clean water—water to fill the basin and drinking pail—had to be carried, a hundred feet when we were lucky, five hundred feet at other times, though finding dirty water was never a problem in our part of the country.

Most houses in Cypress were one of two types: a square made of four smaller squares or a three-room shotgun. Cypress being a lumber town from its inception, all houses were built strong if plain, of good woods and with interiors of beaded-heart pine. When we first arrived in town, we lived in a four-room house on block eleven. But the mustard-colored house was an exception to the rule: a two-story, one of only a few in town—the others owned by Charles Segrist and by the town doctor, Dr. Danger. The construction of our new house on the edge of Cypress was nearing completion. It had seven rooms and an entrance from the front porch into the living room. It had a dining room separate from the living room, and it contained our first bathroom, with a bathing tub and sink that used running water. The toilet would still be outside, though, where my father—who otherwise took easily and perhaps even too eagerly to new things—said it belonged. The conviction that indoor toilets were a misguided notion that would soon pass overrode his otherwise potent desire to join the next class and the next decade. The decision had greatly disappointed my sister Luta, who was anxious to try out a water closet like the one I had used once when paying a call on the Dangers and which Mrs. Danger referred to, eyes cast to the floor, as a commode.

When we arrived home from checking on the crews, my mother was putting pieces of the evening meal on the table. Being Saturday, the food would be simple and eaten early, which my mother said left room in us for the Lord and Sunday dinner both.

She set down a plate of sliced bread as my father and I

walked in, as always holding her back and neck erect, a posture I had noticed other tall women did not trouble with. My mother was an even six feet, level with my father, with a frame that was large if you looked at her front-on but thin as a pipe, except for the swell of bosom, if you saw her from one side or the other. She looked that afternoon as she always did: dark hair knotted at the nape of her neck, a placid warmth in her blue eyes and wide face. My father looked at me and smiled. We shared a knowledge that no one else in town seemed to have discovered: my mother was a beautiful woman.

Emily and Pal were already sitting at the table, waiting to be served, which seemed fair enough in Emily's case. Luta was carrying food and the utensils to eat it with to the table, which was crafted from a single cedar plank taken from the largest tree I had ever seen either standing or felled. Luta set down a terrine holding a stew of potatoes with a little ham from the bone. She emptied the last mason jar of the previous summer's peas into a bowl—bone china but chipped and therefore not used on other days of the week.

A big smile marshaled Luta when she saw us. "And to think we were going to eat supper without you," she said.

Emily looked up only then. "We would never eat without Louis and Daddy."

"I know you wouldn't, honey." My father stroked Emily's straight hair and then gave Pal's head a little knock, which Pal tried to duck but could not.

I smiled at Emily as she squinted her almost-black eyes to take in our father. Unlike tall, clear, light-eyed Luta, Emily had smallness and dark beauty, leaving my father to speculate that there might be more than a few drops of French blood in the family—the blood that made men seek proximity to Dr. Danger's wife, whom the doctor had chosen from a house of pretty girls in Banville.

Emily pulled the crock of stew close to her and breathed its steam, nodding in recognition. Her other senses being opaque—serving more to shield her from the world than to grant her access to it or it to her—she lived in a world mostly of smell.

Her feeble eyesight allowed her to study carefully the back of a beetle but not to recognize her own brother across a room, much less a town square. Her hearing was equally faint, giving her a further distance from the world, something I'd noticed when she was a baby. She'd grown tired of asking people to repeat their words, so she'd taken to ignoring most people while guessing the wishes of those few she was close to. Sometimes she brought me things I hadn't asked for. Because she usually figured right or brought me things just as I realized I wanted them, I always thanked her and accepted the book or letter opener or feather from her hands, hands that were small and cool to the touch even on hot evenings.

The summer before, Emily had lost her sense of taste for several weeks and had barely been able to eat because of it. It was then that she'd learned to inhale the steam of food deeply enough to arouse the memory of taste. Later, when I learned that smell is our most mnemonic sense—the sense that most readily and fully invokes vivid memories—it was easy for me to believe.

Emily's taste buds reawakened after their dormant month, but she continued to derive more pleasure from breathing food than eating it. She never regained the weight she'd lost, and my mother considered it dangerous for her to miss a single meal. My mother even softened her otherwise absolute adherence to the adage that, while colds could be fed, fevers must be starved. Ever-cold Emily rarely succumbed to fevers, but on those occasions when her forehead was warm she was put to bed, but not without food.

I'd read once—in a magazine at the dentist's office—about a man who worked as a perfume expert. This man's olfactory powers were so potent and so refined that he could pick out the tones of more than two hundred flowers and forty spices. The discovery of the New World, the article said, had doubled the scents available to the crafters of perfume. When I read that, I thought for the first time that maybe there was a place in this world for Emily, perhaps a place for every person.

But there was a troubling consequence: Emily's intricate sense of smell made her uncomfortable with her own odor. She'd whispered to me—and I believe to me alone—that her body always smelled sour to her. I told her that it wasn't so, that she smelled the same as everyone and likely better than most. Yet she continued to wash more frequently than any other member of the family, and I often saw her rubbing fresh pine needles or cuttings of lavender hard across the skin of her arms, legs, even the delicate skin of her neck.

Over supper that evening, Luta told us about basketball practice. She was certain that her team would beat the team from

Banville the following week, but she was angry at the coach for moving her to center, on account of her height, when she wanted to play forward.

Pal talked on about one thing and another the way he usually did, tilting his head from side to side as he spoke. I'd tried to tell him that everything that happened to him was not necessarily of great general interest and that not everyone was charmed by his curly hair. Tonight, though, I was quieted by the knife that had been set at my place. It was an ordinary dinner knife indistinguishable from the others save that its blade was missing a crescent-shaped sliver. It was a small shape, yet for me it was the geometry of guilt. I was responsible for the defect.

When we'd been living in the converted passenger car, Luta, Pal, and I had often played underneath it. Using kitchen knives and spoons smuggled outside, we dug miniature tracks. Cola bottles and bits of board stood in as locomotives and flat cars in our artificial representation of our real world. One day, for no reason I can remember save sheer impulse, I threw a knife. I realized, too late, that it was sailing in the direction of Emily, who liked to sit under a tree near us while we played. When I could discern that the knife's arc was too short to endanger Emily, I felt a relief so great that I said aloud the word *God,* in whom I still believed. The knife instead struck a steel rail, chipping the blade improbably. Pal had only recently recovered from one of his many childhood diseases—pellagra this time, caused by his picky appetite. Knowing that he, both younger and sickly, would not be punished, I blamed the chipped knife on him.

After a few weeks, the sight of the knife was like the sound of

Poe's telltale heart, and I confessed. My mother did not punish me, nor did she tell my father, who would have. But she never replaced the knife, not even after we could readily afford a whole new setting. Whenever the knife was placed at my dinner seat, I wondered if my mother was angry with me, or disappointed, or for some reason reminding me to take responsibility for my decisions.

But that Saturday, it was Luta who had set the table, and she was singularly incapable of calculation.

"Louis," she said now, her face as broad and clear as fine-sanded lumber and showing no displeasure, "tell us about your day."

My father's eyes met mine, and my throat tightened. I concentrated to fill in the details of the day without telling about the excitement. I mentioned the progress of several crews but, fearing to venture too close to the truth lest I travel all the way there, not Rabbit's.

I'd always been a reasonably convincing liar, knowing as I did just the right amount of detail to pack around each mistruth. This is not to say that I was a good liar, though, because I was always compelled, later if not sooner, to fess up, just as I had about the damaged knife. I could not stand to have my lies believed. Having my lies accepted by others made me feel, at least some of the time, that I myself was not real, that my true experiences were fiction and had never really happened. And so even as a young man I believed that it's important to get things right, to be accurate inasmuch as that is ever possible.

This time, though, I felt justified in lying. It would have been wrong to upset my mother, who had worried terribly about my father's safety during the trapper wars and even more since my uncle had been killed by a bootlegger.

My father rescued me, interrupting my report to ask my mother what color she wanted the new house painted.

As always before she answered a direct question, she looked down at her hands before she moved to speak. "I have always thought it would be nice to live in a yellow house." She must have anticipated the response, because she added in her gentle, legible voice, "Not a harsh yellow like this house, but a pale, pretty yellow that puts you in mind of Easter."

"Absolutely not." My father's voice was loud enough to startle Emily. "The house needs to be a color that makes a statement, that says something about us and our place in this town."

My mother's mouth curled slightly as it did before one of her rare smiles, but no smile followed. "Something about us. What color did you have in mind?"

"I don't know yet, but I do know it isn't yellow."

He moved on to the subject of the stove for the new house, which would be ordered by mail from a catalogue. The page my father had dog-eared was not the same one on which my mother had lingered. She favored a simpler model, not just because of the price, she said, but so she would already know how to use it.

"Nonsense. You'll learn the new kind in no time. I want you to have the best. I am making enough money now that we don't have to live like where we came from."

"Yes," my mother answered without looking down to her hands first. "And you are spending it just as fast."

I concentrated hard on the design at the bottom of my almost-empty stew bowl: a small blue iris, which I had learned in Miss Fontenot's French translation class was the basis of the fleur-de-lis. Luta began humming "Faith of our Fathers" as loud as a hum can be and fast. She stood to clear the dishes, although Pal was still moving food around the rim of his bowl.

Later that night, I went out back with our dog, a small wire-haired terrier named Terrebone, to feed Buck, the small deer fawn that my father had found abandoned and taken for a pet. I checked that Buck's pen was secured for the night. Usually I just emptied the scrap bucket over the fawn's grains, but this night I held the bucket up to its muzzle, stroking the wild-born animal between its ears when it paused. The crickets and cicadas sounded as loud and orchestrated as any choir and seemed to give movement to the whole outdoors.

Back inside, I settled into my room to read the book that was absorbing me: an illustrated translation of Pliny's notebooks, a book I hoped would guide my own project and that had me plotting an occupation other than the one my father had marked out for me. Though my own project focused on natural history as we now think of it—botany, zoology, geology, meteorology—I was at that time reading Pliny's seventeenth book, which focuses on cultivated trees. In the book, he records his observations on the effects of weather on trees, nutrition through soil and manure, and instructions for planting, grafting, and protecting a tree against caterpillars by having a woman beginning her monthly period walk around each tree with bare feet and an unfastened girdle. I laughed at Pliny for recording superstitions as empirical fact. Yet I could not put out of my mind the image of a shoeless young woman circling a cypress tree, an image that still imprints my dreams. I can also still see the small color reproduction of an engraving done by an Italian artist to illuminate an early copy of Pliny's manuscript. In it, Nero stands before four cultivated trees, holding not a violin but a sword and an orb, pointing down as a whole city disappears into flame.

That night, as my eyelids drooped with my reading, I heard my father leave for his Saturday-night rounds, a job that consisted mainly of making sure there was no out-of-hand fighting at the social club just past the edge of town or at the tunk down in the Negro quarter, which on Saturday night featured a piano player and dancing in addition to food and drink.

Every week my mother waited up for his return, the stories of celebratory gunshots that sometimes veered low giving her worry. I knew, also, that a more real threat came from outside town. My father had made statements against the bootleggers who streamed up by boat and by truck from the Gulf, through what he thought of as his parish, carrying their barrels and their bottles to ever-thirsty New Orleans.

When I folded the book closed over Nero's face, bizarrely serene as Rome is destroyed below him, and extinguished my reading lamp, a rectangle of light from my mother's lamp framed my too-small door.

✦ ✦ ✦

Its easy slope from the Missouri to the Gulf of Mexico might trick an amateur natural historian early in his work into thinking that the massive volume of water moves almost lazily under southern humidity. But no one who has examined the lower Mississippi River, and really no one who has ever looked upon it with concentration, watched its weird movements for longer than an hour, can deny that its cardinal feature is turbulence.

Variations in temperature, wind direction, and air moisture, uneven velocities by depth or breadth, the crooked effects of banks and bed, tidal influences as far north as Baton Rouge, and the river's incredible sediment load like the cast-off weight of the whole country churning its way through the bowel of Louisiana—all these do their strange work. These and other forces spawn eddies, generate spiraling holes capable of swallowing and never releasing full-grown bulls and large horses. Sometimes currents half the width of the river run upstream against its chief force for meters on end.

Such definitive turbulence has long confounded the engineering know-how that brought under control the Missouri, the Po, and the Rhine. Though my life span has made banal the mysteries of large swaths of space-time and the intricacies of subatomic particles—has made the world both bigger and smaller than members of an earlier generation could have imagined—the Mighty Muddy still resists our best math and science.

✦ ✦ ✦

On Sunday, Luta, Emily, and I went to church with our irreligious father while our pious mother stayed home to prepare our meal. As he did every second or third Sunday, Pal complained of stomach pain and was allowed to stay home.

Though by this time I had two sets of good clothes, I put on the suit I'd worn the previous week. My father dressed like Charles Segrist when he arrived straight from New Orleans and the same as Dr. Danger when he attended church. The clothes didn't fall the same way on my father, though, owing to his long neck and arms and the fact that his clothes were mail-ordered and not tailor-made. And his watch chain was only plated with gold and not precious to the core. He could not have afforded Charles Segrist's watch chain, of course, but he would gladly have paid to have his suit done up by a good tailor. He was, however, unwilling to travel to New Orleans to have it fitted.

"This is my pond," he'd said more than once to Charles Segrist.

I understood, even then, that my father had moved up in the world far more than would have been conceivable to his illiterate parents. To climb further out of his childhood was beyond even his own conception. My father had never heard, except a couple of times on the radio, a man who didn't speak with some kind of Southern accent. He'd never heard of the city where I now live, though in it resides one of the world's most famous universities.

Still, my father would be better dressed than anyone else at church, unless Dr. Danger appeared, which happened less and less frequently the longer he was married to his Catholic wife.

The church itself was simple—a rectangle constructed of pine, whitewashed outside but unfinished within—and I puzzle even now at the effort people made to obtain and wear good clothes. On that Sunday, the church was no less full than usual, which is to say it was nearly full but everyone had a seat. The service was uncharacteristically brief. There were no baptisms, and only two people rose to witness. One was an old woman who spoke every week, telling us more often than not that there were two generations of God and that just because we had an offer of forgiveness and salvation from the loving New Testament Son, we shouldn't assume that His Old Testament Father wouldn't smite us where we stood, sinners that we all were. There were a few enthusiastic "Amens" after she returned to her seat, but we'd all heard it before, and even the most pious worshippers crave variation. The other person to step forward that day was a man in his twenties made penitent from several nights of heavy drinking, a binge stopped, he told us, by a visit from Jesus, to whom he had promised that he would never again set foot in the Sodom and Gomorrah that was New Orleans.

In the weeks that followed, as the rain drenched Cypress Parish and seemingly the whole country and the river swelled high against its levees, there would be a great deal of fervent witnessing at the Cypress Baptist Church. Yet the number of souls willing to douse themselves for salvation would remain steady and small, and at the time it made sense to me that some folks, rain-weary as we all were, would prefer flame to water. It's commonly believed that trial and threat bring about conversion, deathbed or otherwise, but in Cypress that year, the saved and unsaved mostly stuck to their chosen paths. It seemed to me that people are not changed by difficulty, risk, or even aging but instead harden into more of their same. I think that's true, but perhaps the explanation is more simple still: the idea of dunking your head under water became increasingly unappealing as the threat of a general baptism by nature grew stronger.

As we walked toward home after church that Sunday, I looked for people I knew. I always liked to run into Gaspar Anderson, but I knew the painter was away on one of his trips to the small islands in the Gulf, from which he would return with dozens of sketches to support his work in the coming weeks, until it was time again to row out in search of more images.

"I'll meet you at home," I told my father and sisters, breaking away to walk past the Catholic church as mass was letting out.

Built from stone atop a high foundation, the church was long and tall but very narrow. With its colored panes of window glass and its long lines, it was much prettier than our church. Yet the dark, fragrant interior I glimpsed as the heavy wooden doors pushed slowly outward was as alien and mysterious as animal sacrifice. I had no idea what people did inside, but to this day the smell of incense is for me the smell of exotic temptation, at once alluring and terrifying.

I panned the human stream descending the steep front steps and tipped my hat to Mrs. Danger. Following close behind her, in a striped jacket and bowler hat, was the dentist. Given that his last name was long and pronounced correctly by no one, he was known as Dr. B. Some thought he was from South America, while a few said that he was just an educated Isleño from

Delacroix Island, which was the end of Louisiana and, many said, the end of the world.

After greeting the dentist, I tipped my hat and nodded to my French-translation teacher, Miss Fontenot. Though my pulse always quickened when the French teacher called on me, and I sometimes found myself watching her at the blackboard when I was supposed to be writing out sentences, I was now looking for only one face: that of Nanette Lançon.

The Lançons had arrived in Cypress scratch-poor, refugees of the 1922 flood. Maybe because of their shabby and sometimes too-small clothes, but probably because they were French and Catholic and victims of nature and simply new, Henri and Nanette Lançon were not accepted by the town's children for a long time. It took longer, even, than it took the family to move from a single rented room in the Washburn boardinghouse into something a good step up from a shack.

Henri had done what some kids will under such circumstances: he became funny. He cracked jokes even when it meant trouble and otherwise, in assorted ways, drew attention to himself. Once, at a Fourth of July pie-eating contest, he ate blackberry-peach pie until he could not pack in another bite. Then he stepped behind a tree and stuck his finger down his throat—to free up room, he said—before downing another half pie and taking the blue ribbon. But relocation was a different experience for Nanette. I knew this for sure because I had watched her. Her approach, so different from her brother's, was enigmatic and ultimately irresistible. She did not seek attention, did not woo others or seek favor. Quiet and studious, she at least pretended not to care, and possibly truly did not, what the rest of the town thought of her. At the end of a school day, she gathered her books to her chest and walked away, eyes already well ahead of her, passing without comment Henri, who was most often at work amusing a pack by walking along a fence top or scaring a squirrel from a tree with a fast rock.

Yet over time, in subtle increments, Nanette was accepted. Perhaps this was simply because the young people of Cypress had finally known her long enough. Or maybe, as they matured, they recognized her prettiness. Their yielding might have derived from the fact that the nursery her father had started from nothing became something and Nanette's dresses got nicer every year. Or perhaps the respect she earned by not trying to make people like her softened into something more socially lucrative than respect. Still, though, she always stood just outside any circle, always seemed to be both listening to the conversation and thinking about something else entirely—something so rare and special that others could not have guessed its nature even if they exerted themselves.

I caught sight of Henri, whose wavy hair was visible over the heads of everyone around him. I looked lower, but upon seeing what I was looking for—Nanette's serenely angled face, full lips, deeply set eyes—I was lost to any action save escape. Nanette placed her soft stare on me, and I could only keep walking.

I circled the block until I came back to the shady park that occupied Cypress's center. It was intended by the lumber company to promote social bonds and provide a place for children to be occupied in adult view but without adult care. A stout bay fidgeted against the other horses at the community post. And, sure enough, when I got close to home, I could see my grandfather's buggy sitting out front, the alternate leg propped on the seat. I always suspected that the visibility of the prosthesis, its downright conspicuousness, was intentional. My grandfather was proud of that fake leg.

He'd done what few do, and the opposite of what my father aimed for. He had reverted to the obsolete, replacing his automobile with the bay-drawn buggy and his finely made prosthesis with a wooden peg. My father had explained the return to horse-and-buggy while teaching me to drive the car we'd acquired from his father-in-law's peculiar choice. The backwardness—my father's term for it—had both economic and social origins: the car was expensive to keep, and the Negro driver had not always been fully welcome, much less comfortable, on the overnight stays essential to the work of a traveling mechanic.

As a younger man, my grandfather had worked in the sawmill that eventually took his right leg. After recovering from the amputation, for which he had been given a good amount of whiskey but no stronger anodyne, he set about building his current business. Now he traveled about from place to place, fixing sewing machines and performing other small mechanical work.

Despite what they had done to his body, or possibly because of it, machines held a deep fascination for him. "Moving parts," he would say, "are things we did not have when I was a boy." He had real genius for their workings. He also invented contraptions: a pulley system for getting his clothes from his chest of drawers to his bedside, a double fan for quickly cooling a room, an ice-cream maker that cranked itself, a specialized nail gun. I've always assumed that my affinity for math came from him and wondered what he might have been in another time and place.

Still, my grandfather always preferred a small to a large machine. Perhaps this bias contributed to his eagerness to forsake the automobile he could not drive one-legged for the horse and buggy he could command alone.

But the second reversion was never explained to me, and I could only guess at my grandfather's reasons for preferring the functional but old and ugly wooden peg to the fine representation of a leg he used now only to shake menacingly at the drivers of slow-moving buggies and cars.

Hidden at first behind my grandfather's buggy, where the old man had unhitched the horse before walking it to the communal posts in the park, was Pal. There he sat on the porch, his cheeks marked with tears now dry, his countenance forlorn in the particular way he had spent long hours cultivating. He stroked Terrebone, who sat with his neck stretched long over Pal's thigh.

I aimed for the door, but as fast as I cleared the threshold my father ordered me, with a look and a certain pronunciation of my name, back out to talk to my brother.

I used my hand to brush off a piece of the porch and sat down next to Pal, Terrebone between us. The dog was so small and gentle that it was hard to reconcile the animal with my father's assertion that Terrebone's jaws were so strong and his little brain so tenacious that you could hoist him up the flagpole and down again without the dog letting go. It was true enough that everyone in the family save Emily—whose sensitive nature was recognized by animals even more than by people—had lost a shoe or a book to the terrier's never-give-up hold.

Finally I said, "Grandpa got your goat?"

Pal nodded, and I could see that he would cry again if he spoke.

"Horse bite?"

Again he nodded, lifting a limp arm to show me the red handprints where our grandfather had twisted his skin in opposite directions over his bicep.

I wanted to ask him why he had skipped church, knowing that our grandfather was expected. I held my comment, though, for the sake of expediency, and instead told him what I had learned about the old man. "He really likes children, Pal. But he tests you. He's a man that endured great pain and survived, and he wants to know that you're made of the same fiber. The important thing is not to cry in front of him and not to run away. Get through one horse bite without crying, and he probably won't do it again. You just have to think about something else while it's happening. Then it's over and you forget about it."

Pal titled his head, and it seemed that, for once, he might be listening to what I had to say.

"What you should do now is go inside, sit right close to him, and ask him to teach you how to Indian count."

"How much will it hurt?"

I had to laugh at that. "It won't hurt even a little."

Inside my grandfather was sitting in my father's armchair, his arms laid on the rests in a way that accentuated the drastic slope of his thick shoulders, seemingly the precise angle of his long, drooping mustache. This posture lent the impression that he was being pulled down by some extrapowerful gravitational force and resisting with the same strength of body and will that had kept his trunk out of the sawmill teeth that had chewed his leg into nothing.

He took in my face with his small blue eyes and nodded. I nudged Pal, who lingered behind me, then shook the old man's hand before going to my room to change out of my suit. My father thought we should keep wearing our good clothes through Sunday dinner, but my mother, who managed the laundering, had subtly prevailed on this one issue.

When I returned in ordinary trousers and a shirt, Pal was in the armchair with our grandfather, who was saying, "One-a-mon, two-a-mon, zickery, zockery, zan. Wickeybone, wack-abone, toleman, ten, e-ho, ank-oh, follygolly, humpshoulder, twenty."

It no longer bothered me that the numbers were off in this counting scheme, that ten was nine and twenty was fourteen. I'd learned by then about numerical systems not based on ten, and sometimes, in a dream, what my grandfather called Indian counting suggested an exquisite mathematical secret that I could almost solve.

Over a large dinner of roast chicken, green beans, and rice with sawmill gravy—which we always called white gravy in front of my grandfather—he told my mother, his daughter, about his most recent travels.

"People are mightily worried about the rain, and I'll tell you this, the newspapers down here aren't reporting half of what's starting to happen upriver. So far it's just backwater flooding, but mark my words, the river's coming and no one's ever going to forget it."

"I suppose there's nothing *just* about backwater flooding if you live on backwater," my mother said softly.

"That's the truth." My father nodded in agreement before turning back to my grandfather. "By the way," he said, speaking from the side of his mouth in an exaggerated way, making his words seem like an overheard secret, "I've been meaning to ask you if that widow in Natchez broke her sewing machine again."

My grandfather laughed, his mirth nearly folding his small eyes into the wrinkles of his face. "Seems like something's wrong with that machine every time I get to town. Only, funny thing is that it works just fine when I go to test it. She's always so very surprised and says I have the magic touch."

"Enough on that subject for the time being," my mother said. She stood to clear the table, and Luta hopped up as well.

"Widow or no, the truth is that the business I'm in will be going by the wayside. It's the catalogues and postmen that are the future. Now if I can't fix something for a few cents, people say they'll just buy a new one. Sometimes buying the whole thing is cheaper than getting just the part they need, and most'd rather have the new model anyhow. The makers are always adding on another fancy gadget or putting in some new kind of bobbin or making a sewing machine that's pink or yellow or some color that ladies want. Just one more thing to break, often as not, which means they can sell the next new model soon enough, too."

"That the truth?" my father asked absently.

"Don't matter so much to me," my grandfather said, adding in a whisper while my mother carried dishes to the kitchen, "Not while I've still got my regular widows."

I smiled at the image of my grandfather being fed at the kitchen tables of lonely women from southern Louisiana to Mississippi.

My father laughed before speaking. "Not a business for a young man to go into, from the sounds of it. But we're going to make a doctor out of Louis, and if I'm not wrong, and I'm usually not, Pal's hands are about soft enough to work in a bank."

"I smell coffee and pie," Emily said. "Chess pie!"

"There's some sly timing for you," my father said when we heard a firm knock at the door. "How come everyone manages to pay calls just as dessert is being served?"

Charles Segrist, who stood at the door hat in had, was invited in. He was one of those rare red-headed men who looks extraordinarily healthy. He was tall and strapping, with color in his face. His eyes, the caramel color of a fox's, looked perpetually amused. His hair, a burnt-orange color streaked with blond, was wavy but smooth and under control, suggestive of the man's polished energy and a taste for life's luxuries, large and small.

"Fresh in from New Orleans?" my father asked between Segrist's first and second slices of pie.

I studied their exchange. Charles Segrist was the only younger man my father ever deferred to, which he did fully but uncomfortably, speaking less often and at less length than he did with other men.

"Indeed I am, William. Which brings me to the point of my call. I had planned to return last night but found myself rather indisposed to drive until after this morning's coffee. I have concluded from this, and from similar instances in the recent past, that I am in need of a driver from time to time. I could use someone who is presentable and can accompany me on errands and such but who indulges a good bit less in sugar and such than I myself do. Now that young Louis here knows how to drive, I consider him the top candidate for the job." He traded his empty pie plate for the cup of coffee Luta poured.

I controlled the muscles of my face, trying not to look eager, but all I could think of was driving Charles Segrist's shiny car through the streets of New Orleans, a city I had seen only in photographs.

Still my father did not answer.

"Given your plans for him to rise in the world," Charles Segrist paused to sip his coffee, "you may agree that this is a good opportunity."

I have never been able to fully like my brother, but when I counseled him that Sunday afternoon, I gave him honest advice. I'd believed what I told him about forgetting pain, believed even that forgetting an unpleasant thing made it the same as though it had never happened. But when events are discounted, a life, like my grandfather's counting system, cannot be totaled. Whenever I heard anyone say that something *doesn't add up,* I always used to say, "Everything adds up if you want it to." But what I think now is that nothing really adds up in the end.

Now that I'm very old, the pieces of my life swim by in fragments, like pieces of a photograph in a fluid. Often I remember what I know or have read about as though it happened to me, while forgetting what I know must have been vivid and crucial moments of my own life.

◆ ◆ ◆

Marcus Garvey was deported from the port of New Orleans in the final month of 1927. He had been released from a Georgia prison where, after losing almost all of his support among the black establishment, he had served part of a federal sentence for fraud.

He had lost by no means all of his support, however, and on the day of his deportation more than five hundred of his followers—many women and children among them—filed along the docks in the unusually cold, driving rain to hear Garvey speak.

From the high deck of the fruit steamship *Saramacca,* which would bear him to Kingston, Jamaica, Garvey spoke: "I desire to convey to my supporters and friends and to the American public in general my heartfelt thanks for the great confidence they have shown in me at all times and especially during the periods of my trial and imprisonment, which I regard as a wonderful testimony of the knowledge they have of my innocence. I leave America fully as happy as when I came, in that my relationship with my people was most pleasant and inspiring, and I shall work forever on their behalf. The program of nationalism is as important now as it ever was, and my entire life shall be devoted to the supreme cause. I sincerely believe that it is only by nationalizing the Negro and awakening him to the possibilities of himself that this universal problem can be solved. Good-bye, America! Farewell, my people!"

Of course his words could not be heard by most of those who suffered the wet cold to raise a wave, but a transcript of his speech was published in numerous papers the following day, together with this final written message from Garvey: "To my white friends I desire to say that I shall always consider their interest in me as a cause for respecting everywhere and always the rights of their Race. The program I represent is not hostile to the white race or any other race. All that I want to do is to complete the freedom of the Negro economically and culturally and make him a full man. The intelligent white man has and will continue to endorse my program."

The rain that fell on Garvey's farewell address reminded many in New Orleans of one winter earlier, when rain was general over much of the country. Rain had come first to the flat states and then stalked the Mississippi River Valley, where, as Garvey spoke, thousands—far more black than white—remained homeless.

The rain had come in August, and it had stayed, the occasional piece of clear sky no more than a short-lived taunt, a reminder of a time before. On the first day of 1927, the Mississippi River measured over flood stage at the important marker at Cairo, Illinois. Never before in recorded history—not even ahead of the momentous flood of 1922—had this event come so early in the year.

✦ ✦ ✦

As the days of latest winter came, went, and gave way to early spring, I continued to work on my natural history while trying to convince my parents to let me drive for Charles Segrist. I made entries on several species of pine and bird, recording also some comparative observations of the movements of bayou and marsh waters.

Increasingly, though, I was preoccupied by the same trepidation I experienced every year and every year swore I would leave behind. My fear of my birthday was irrational, but it was long-lived and not completely without foundation. Though of course there was no cause-and-effect relationship, it was the case that some bad thing or another—sometimes full tragedy—often coincided with my birthday or fell close to it.

I don't know if I truly remember the first such event through the murky memory veil of young childhood or know about it only because I heard it told later. It had to do with a family friend named Scotter, who was called to war around my birthday.

Scotter had been tall and gangly—my mother always compared him to a bean needing stringing—and he'd told me that his height would save him. "Never you worry, little man," he'd said. "Even if the Germans sink my ship, my legs are long enough to touch the ocean floor and keep me from drowning. I'll just have to walk home, that's all."

One year later, on my birthday, we heard the news that Scotter's boat had been torpedoed. For some days, I waited for him to walk into town with his pants soaked to his thighs but no higher. Then my father told me what everyone else already knew: Scotter's legs were unusually but not preternaturally long, and the ocean's water was deeper than I could imagine.

Maybe it was two, maybe three years later that another friend of the family—a man who was a barber by trade and who my father said gave him his last good haircut—was robbed and killed while visiting kin in Macomb, Mississippi.

It was a year after that death that a well-liked switchman, whose proper name I never knew but whom everyone called Lefty, died when his foot slipped as he opened a railway coupling for junction with the engine. He fell between the two couplings and was crushed.

I remember what my father told my mother: "Damnedest thing was that he was conscious of what was happening to him, right into the moment he passed over. I almost thought he was going to be able to tell us what he saw on the other side. I almost thought he was going to."

Then, of course, there was my Uncle Walter's death, which happened on the day before my fifteenth birthday. At the time he was killed, my uncle was a sheriff in a neighboring parish. One day—and it was day, bright in the afternoon—he arrested a trapper accused of smuggling liquor north. The accused was a local man who gave no resistance. It was said later that my uncle was too casual about taking him in. He didn't frisk the man properly, and when he looked away for a moment, stopping to greet a woman whose husband he knew, the trapper pulled a pistol and shot him through the head. My uncle dropped on the spot, dead.

The next day, which was my birthday, my family boarded the passenger train that carried my uncle's body in its luggage car.

Luta was the only one who cried as we watched the casket unloaded to a flat-bodied, steel-wheeled baggage wagon and pulled by a railroad man to the horse-drawn buggy that waited.

A few months later, in a book borrowed from school, I read about the journey of Abraham Lincoln's body, by train, from the national capital to his boyhood home in Illinois. Because of my uncle's funeral, I thought I knew what that might have been like, and for my entire life I have thought of my uncle whenever someone mentions Lincoln.

The trapper who killed Walter Proby turned himself in immediately and apologized, saying he didn't know what had come over him. He was used to the open air, he said, and had lost his mind over the idea of being locked up somewhere small. He preferred to be hanged, he said, and he was granted his choice. My father wanted us all to go see the hanging, but my mother convinced him to take only me.

Some years, Cypress Parish went all winter without frost, and children played in short pants on Christmas afternoon. Yet I had seen snow twice in my life, and I knew from my own observations that a late freeze was possible in any year. After the early warm stretch, 1927 was noticeably cooler than normal.

Drawing more on the faith than the recklessness of youth, I risked the weather, gathering from the hothouse behind Buck's pen the seeds and seedlings and cuttings I'd been collecting from vacant lots, the clippings I'd been given by my mother's friend, and several plants purchased from the Lançon nursery. I hauled them by wagon, my elbow stretched behind me as I made my way over to the new house. I would have avoided the direct route if I had not been pulling a loaded wagon because it took me in front of the big store. Owned but rented out by the Washburn sisters, the store was still a place of small shame for me. On most days, I took the longer route, not minding the extra distance to avoid the guilty reminder.

The incident that embarrassed me had occurred only a few days after we'd moved to Cypress. I could no longer reconstruct my motivation, or maybe I never understood why I had done it. Perhaps I thought I was important because of my father's new job, or perhaps I just wanted the slingshot—the store's last—that the black boy was reaching for.

I'd told the store's proprietor, and later my parents, that I had shoved the boy because he had breathed in my face, that I could feel the humidity of it on my cheek, that his breath was rank.

I was not punished. My father simply said, "Don't cause trouble for people who can't defend themselves." At the time I protested, saying that the boy was bigger than I was even if he was a little younger. My father said, "Talking when you should be thinking will make you stupid. Keep thinking about what I've told you." Of course, I eventually came to understand why the boy had not shoved back and what my father had meant.

As always, I felt relieved when the store was half a block behind me, and I enjoyed the rest of the walk to the new house. With its foundations set into a man-made swell of mounded earth, the house was higher than the street. Even unpainted and not quite finished, it looked imposing.

The bed I had prepared was in the side yard. It was blocked from clear street view by the large azalea bushes my father had ordered from the Lançons' nursery and Henri had planted in the front. But it would still be sunny enough.

In the damp and good-smelling soil, using a small trowel and my hand, I planted the things I had brought, most of them herbs and flowers remarkable for their scent: lemon balm and verbena, mallow, creeping thyme, rosemary, honeysuckle, several kinds of lavender, a geranium that smelled more like gardenia. Closing my eyes and inhaling deeply, I pictured Emily, a rubbed leaf held to her nose, a smile whispering across her pretty face.

I wanted her to know that the new house was her home.

On my way back, my hands brushed dry but still stained with dark earth, I swung by the Washburn women's boardinghouse. It had been the Lançon family's first home in Cypress. They had squeezed into a room there—a kindness on the part of Betsy Washburn and her shy sister and one that was repaid as the Lançons flourished. From the day Jules Lançon opened his nursery, the Washburn house never lacked for spring flowers or for poinsettias at Christmas.

Most of the boardinghouse tenants were not down-on-their-luck families but solitary men: men without families at all, or men living apart from families for one reason or another. Dr. B, the dentist—who was understood to be from Chile or from Argentina or from some other country where Spanish is spoken and where summer is winter—lived there for years. "I have not the wife nor the time to keep a house," he told those who asked. "It is convenient for me to live here, and my room is sunny."

When Dr. B did buy a house, there was ample speculation on one side of the town gossip that he planned to marry and on the other side that he wished to have his own space in which to entertain ladies, emphasis on the plural. Some of the local men who did have wives went to considerable trouble and expense, when those wives complained of a toothache, to take them to dentists in Grenada or even New Orleans. I'd heard my father use the term *ladies' man,* and I had overheard it said that those wives who did see the local dentist were sometimes noticed to develop tooth trouble rather more frequently than is common. When I was younger, I'd given little thought to what lay behind such talk, and for my part, I liked going to the dentist, so long as it didn't involve drilling, because of the magazines in the anteroom and the dentist's tales of life lived elsewhere.

Sometimes men who traveled for the lumber company roomed at the boardinghouse. Once, a mysterious man had stayed there for four days before my father found out he was in town to organize workers for an international union. My father beat the spit out of him, waited while he fetched his case and settled his account, and then escorted him past the edge of town.

"I told him there would be no hard feelings so long as he didn't ever come back," my father had said to my mother. "I even told him good luck—I like to see poor men rise up as much as anyone—but not in Cypress."

Aside from the dentist, the most illustrious boardinghouse tenant was Gaspar Anderson, the painter. From several parishes over, he called Cypress home because it offered him—in addition to the quiet life he preferred by habit and commitment to his art—easy access to the offshore islands whose birds and trees he considered his life's work to capture in color.

Though people in Cypress believed this was a peculiar life's work, they liked Gaspar. Refusing as he did to move into shade if the comfort cost him an angle on his subject, and spending hours oaring to and from the islands in his metal rowboat, he was bleached and tanned, his fair hair streaked almost white and his skin a nutty color. His voice, clean and moderate, was sonorous, and for this he was liked by women. Men approved of his ruggedness and his reputation for plain speech and cash-only dealings. They said he was a straight-up fellow.

I liked him for many reasons, including the fact that he was one of the only men I knew who had gone to college, and he was the only person I'd ever met who had been to Europe for any reason other than war. He was the only person in my orbit who knew about art or the history of faraway places, and the only person I regularly saw reading a book for pleasure. Perhaps because I was not quite a man, I imagined the painter was older than he was. But my perception of Gaspar as wise and worthy of confidence stemmed more from the things he said than from any maturity measurable by years.

I walked more slowly when I neared the boardinghouse, and, sure enough, Gaspar's bleached head stuck through his second-floor window.

"I can't stop working now," he called out. "But let's go down to the river when you're out of school tomorrow."

✦ ✦ ✦

By the end of 1926, tributaries flooded parts of Nebraska, South Dakota, Oklahoma, Kansas, Illinois, Kentucky, West Virginia, Tennessee, and Arkansas. Every single gauge on the Ohio River, the Missouri River, and the Mississippi River recorded the highest water ever measured. Early in the following year, Pittsburgh and Cincinnati flooded, and the U.S. Weather Bureau observed no fewer than ten distinct crests carrying themselves into the lower Mississippi.

In February, localized flooding killed dozens of people in the state of Mississippi. The count of dead and homeless began then in earnest and soon dwarfed itself.

Still it rained everywhere. In one day—a day that should have been unique but was not—nearly six inches of rain drenched already saturated New Orleans, a city built mostly on land lower than sea level.

It would not be long before sandbags were scarce and every levee from the northern tip of the Yazoo-Mississippi Delta south to the Gulf of Mexico was patrolled by men prepared to—and in some cases most eager to—shoot saboteurs through the heart.

✦ ✦ ✦

I disliked having my mouth worked on as much as anyone, but even as a teenager, I preferred getting quickly past unpleasantness over forestalling the inevitable. And while I waited for Dr. B to finish with another patient, I was glad to thumb through the stack of magazines, seeing how people up North dressed, reading about up-and-coming politicians, skimming financial advice as though I had money to invest, and reading the often oblique cartoons.

I wasn't surprised to find one about a Southerner who missed his train because he couldn't understand that 8:45 is when the clock's hands point toward 9. I knew that Southerners were a joke in the North, and I mostly believed that it was true that we were behind the times, that we were poorer and attended schools that were not up to snuff. More than anything, I wanted to study science at Harvard or Yale or Miami University—somewhere where it snowed every winter, where ivy grew up brick, where everyone read books and no one thought it was strange to look through a microscope.

Though I loved the bayous and swamps and even the summer's heat, and though I felt a strong affinity for the trees and birds I could name without a reference book—the species I was recording and describing in my natural history—I knew even then that someday I would move away to a place that was colder, a place with fewer insects and snakes, a place of higher ground and less water.

Mrs. Danger, the doctor's wife, passed me on her way out through the waiting room, nodding but not stopping to make conversation when I rose to open the door for her. Her eyes were damp, and I hoped my own procedure would be less painful.

Standing in the doorjamb between the anteroom and his office, Dr. B pressed his fingertips together as he watched Corinne Danger leave. His coat was off and his shirtsleeves were rolled up, but as always, his clothing was elegant and looked expensive. "Louis," he said roundly and with a faint accent, "sorry to have kept you waiting. Please come in."

While he drilled and filled a cavity in one of my molars, his metal instruments caught glinting light and made small, somehow comforting clinking sounds. He spoke of the delicious custard apples and other fruits of South America, the beauty of a river near his home, a woman he knew who could sing more beautifully than anyone he had ever heard on the radio.

I did my best to make noises of approval or at least interest, but mostly I listened with my mouth wet and wide open. When he asked me if I'd ever been in love, I tried to make a sound that was noncommittal.

"You have the look of a man in love." He smiled down at me, his neat mustache spreading a little. "Where I come from, everyone understands that love is the most important thing. A man gives up everything for love and is never sorry for it. He never regrets it. Never."

I sat up to spit and asked Dr. B to remind me of the city he came from. Settled back into the chair, mouth again agape, I listed to stories of Santiago until he pulled the cotton from my gums and told me I was free to return to school.

✦ ✦ ✦

During the early 1970s and with the best of intentions, a program was established to train young and poor black women in the parish northeast of Cypress to be dental hygienists. Money and volunteer time were corralled, promising candidates were recruited, and a class of sixteen young women emerged prepared for jobs that were better paying than their other options of working as maids, filleting at the local catfish-processing plant, or—and this was the alternative that most concerned that parish's white residents—subsisting on government money.

Not one woman was placed in a job, however. A local dentist, off the record, explained: "I would love to have helped out by hiring one, but my clients don't want black fingers in their mouths. They should have trained those girls for something besides touching people's mouths."

✦ ✦ ✦

Many years after I left Cypress and was well into the midde part of what has been a long life, I developed a strand of chaos theory that my colleagues, even those who did not like me personally, hailed as something new and important. Though it took a long time to germinate, I could date the insight behind my formulation to the first time I stared hard at the Mississippi River.

Perhaps what made this moment of seeing critical, when it might have proved fleeting and without consequence, was the fact that it occurred only weeks before the river swelled as never before or since, taking its high toll on life and limb and livelihood. It occurred only weeks before the river swelled and changed forever my knowledge of life and how it is lived.

Emily sat several yards upriver, sorting shells. Her face was turned into the breeze, and the mild wind lifted her hair as a single wide ribbon. I made a place for myself on the cut flat of the levee top, between Emily and the spot Gaspar had chosen to set up his easel.

While Gaspar painted, I tried to describe in my notebook what I saw. The water was high—of that there could be no doubt—but I had seen it as high before. Yet I had never seen the river move so swiftly or with so much internal turmoil. Never before had I felt the levee shimmy under me as it did then. I had twice seen unmoored cows sucked down into the mysterious darkness of the river, but never had I seen a whirlpool so large as the one that now churned before me. It was a cauldron capable of making not only a heifer but a large house, or perhaps even something more, disappear from human sight.

I jotted down an estimate of the river's overall velocity, but I knew the figure was useless. The river contained so many speeds, in so many directions at once, that an average number held no meaning. I scanned the great brown width and noted the relative distance of back currents and eddies. I tried to determine which upstream rivulet was mostly tide.

"I shouldn't think you'd need anything on your palette but brown and a little green," I called to Gaspar.

"Then look closer," the painter answered.

My pen now loose in my hand, I tried to see the river as Gaspar saw it. "White," I said, "in the froth of the waves."

Gaspar paused from his work. "And gaze at the whirlpool. There's blue there and black and even pink."

I nodded. "I can see them now." I felt on my face the moisture of the rain about to fall.

"You have the eyes of a scientist, not a painter." Gaspar wiped his brush with the blue cloth that usually hung from his belt and was now smeared with dozens of shades of color, most of them green. The move was efficient, one so long practiced it seemed unconscious. "You make observations," he said. "You describe the river by adding the sum of its parts, perhaps even contemplate the laws of nature that make it what it is. The river has no effect on you. What I set down is an interpretation. My picture is mine, not what someone else might see. And it is most certainly not the river. It is my painting of the river, which is a lot but also nothing."

I combed for something that might sound intelligent but also diplomatic. "I believe the river defies all of our efforts to capture it."

Gaspar laughed and dipped his brush, quickly and just barely, into a glob of white paint, then deeper into black, adding the smallest amount of red to the resulting dark gray. "That may be what the artist has in common with the scientist. We know our best efforts are doomed to be approximations. We have awe for our subjects of study, know that they are more than we are. It's the engineers who have all the answers."

"My father said if it wasn't for the engineers, we'd be flooded out every year."

"Well, we're certainly sitting on engineering right now, so your father may well be right. But I know this: I know that it's always a mistake to believe you can control something wild." He paused, then added, "Of course it's likely a mistake not to try anyway."

I looked far upriver, where I knew that storm upon storm had dumped more rain than anyone alive could ever remember and where it rained still. In the foreground of my field of vision, Emily pressed shards of shell into the skin of her arm. I walked to her.

Standing over her in the gathering wind, I saw the impressions in her arm. They looked like fossils embedded in flat shale—an image of former life preserved—except that the marks were red, like the segmented curve of burn left by the buck moth caterpillars that sometimes fell from the oaks in the Cypress central square.

"Louis." Emily's whisper was carried rather than smothered by the wind, and it sounded to me like chimes. "I can smell the rain of a dozen different towns. All their rain is in the river. I can smell those towns. I smell a boy, a girl."

She smiled as she pulled a sharp piece of oyster shell across the inner crook of her elbow, drawing a beaded line of blood.

I squatted at her side and gently took the shell from her hand. "Tell me what else you smell," I said, stroking her thick, smooth hair as she straightened her arm to study the dotted blood that now marked it.

"A boy, a girl," she repeated. "A dog, a carnival, a mother." She lifted her face toward the river, smiled, and continued the litany. "A road that nobody uses, pickles, a gasoline car, flowers, a game being played by dogs. And something bad, too, something I don't know a name for."

From behind us, Gaspar said, "And Emily has another way of seeing the river. I don't know what hers is called. Not art, not science, something else."

I stood straight, surprised to be annoyed that Gaspar had crept up on us. "But that's just it," I said, hearing points in my words. "It isn't a way of seeing. She uses another sense."

The artist gazed at Emily the way I had seen him look at a tree he might paint, and I saw my sister in true color against the steel-flat sky. I saw the dark blue and brown in her black hair, the pink and pearly blue glowing through the sallow translucence of her skin. I saw the small green leaves embroidered on her white shift, the smudges of red and brown dirt on her bare, narrow feet.

"We should go home now," I said. And I stood close at my sister's side while Gaspar packed his materials into the small wooden suitcase he so often carried.

✦ ✦ ✦

The sole surviving finished work of Pliny the Elder is his *Historia Naturalis*. Including detailed descriptions of lands, rivers, animals, plants, stones, buildings, and works of art, it is an encyclopedic compendium of the known beliefs—many but by no means all of them fact—of the Roman world of his day.

Subsequent scholars have noted that the thirty-seven volumes of Pliny's natural history contain little original work. Indeed, Pliny himself freely admitted that his work drew not only or even chiefly on his own observations but rather on multiple sources. These sources included both published authorities of the day and the overheard reports of people who had seen, with their own eyes, sea monsters.

✦ ✦ ✦

Nanette Lançon had seen everything on the boats that had carried her family from all that she knew and that her parents thought of as good. She had seen far too much.

She had witnessed those things everyone had. She had seen the dogs stranded on roofs, some of which barked for days and then weeks, waning into their rib cages, smart enough to drink brackish floodwater but too creaturely dumb or water-scared or overwhelmed by magnitude to swim to food.

She had seen other things, too, things that she and maybe no one else saw. Those were the things she wouldn't speak of, the things I try to imagine on days when I'm feeling strong of mind. I have tried to fathom the forces that determined what she did and who she became, to wonder who she might have become had our lives been different.

Every society has its optimists and pessimists, its idealists and its pragmatists, but which group is most sane varies by circumstance. Even back then, I was conscious that Nanette's view of the world was different from that of those of us who didn't know what she knew. And so it was that my little card of pluses and minuses—pros and cons, strengths and weaknesses, worthy attributes and flaws, light and dark, good and evil—touched her more deeply than I had hoped.

Several days after I planted Emily's scent garden and a couple of days after I sat at the river with Emily and Gaspar, Miss Fontenot handed out blank paper cards and instructed us to write, in French, "Three good qualities and three wanting areas" about each of our classmates.

"We can all benefit," she explained, "from checking our

opinions of ourselves against what others think of us. Sometimes we overestimate our own characters, but just as often we find that people like us more than we realize. Besides, it will be a nice break from copying out the Proust."

As always, Miss Fontenot's brown hair was parted far to the side and worn long, curled only at the bottom. With a nose that turned up just slightly, heart-shaped lips, obvious cheekbones, and clear skin, she could be described only as very pretty. I knew I was not the only boy in school who tried to please her, though it was true that some of the others sought her attention in less constructive ways than the devoted conjugation of French verbs.

Being who I was, I took the assignment more somberly than some of my smirking friends. For a boy named Luke, I wrote the French words for *funny, unpretentious, charismatic,* in part to impress Miss Fontenot with my vocabulary. I flipped the card over and wrote *dilettante, underachieving, not ambitious*. For Luta's friend Helen, I wrote the terms for *cheerful, dependable,* and *friendly* and then, on the other side, *not studious, provincial, wants to marry young*. For Henri, I wrote *funny, good-hearted, daring* and *acts like a circus clown, eats like a pig, tricky*.

The card for Nanette took the longest. I'd saved it for last, which was a well-intended if not a good idea. As the clock ticked away the seconds in loud, uneven bursts that kept accurate time only in average, in ticks that were at once slower and faster in a manner that defied what I already knew about physics, it proved to have been a misjudgment. On the positive side of the card, I wrote *intelligente, jolie, bienveillante aux les animaux*. Immediately,

I wished I had written *elegant,* which would have better conveyed the great respect I felt for how Nanette comported herself, rather than *jolie,* the more common word that could have described any of several girls in the room.

Nanette sat several rows in front of me and to the left. I studied the soft down on her arm, the way her dark curls splayed over her shoulder, the line of her neck showing through those curls. But I could not, from my angle, see her face.

Under the duress of passing time, I wrote on the card's flip side, forgetting even to translate my ideas into French: *knows she's smart, knows she's pretty.* As I thought of anything at all for the third negative, anything that was not cruel—perhaps a way to word the dark side of *kind to animals*—I scrawled *too soft natured.* Miss Fontenot collected the cards, taking my card for Nanette from my hand before I could fix it.

Henri looked around at all of us, grinning. A few of us peered here and there cautiously or avoided making eye contact altogether, but most seemed unaffected by the exercise. I realized that I had taken the task too seriously, that I had mistaken accuracy for true understanding and made a mistake.

I left school that day without speaking to anyone, taking relief in the fact that Nanette would not know which card was mine. But even as I told myself this, I knew it wasn't true. The *bienveillante aux les animaux* made the card unique, marked it with my identity more, even, than did my weakly disguised handwriting.

She would, I knew, remember our only real encounter, when I had come upon her trying to free a trapped muskrat. She would remember how she had permitted me to see her tears. She would remember how she had told me about the cows that squeezed each other to death in their crazed effort to place four hooves on wood, about the horse that had stepped on a child's head, about the other horrors she had seen on the boat that had saved her life.

I hated the idea that she might never again speak to me, much less confide in me. Still young and not yet as selfish as we all become as adults, I hated even more the idea that my words might cause her any pain.

The entries I made in my natural history were simple lists of details with the occasional threat of teenaged philosophy clumsily knitted in. They were also the beginning of something: the first stutters of a life of science.

Yet they were also a postponement—a holding still of what I saw, a stalling of life by a young man who fancied that he understood the composition of a pine tree but had yet to acquire even a rudimentary comprehension of human motivation.

Or so Gaspar Anderson tried to tell me one day when I visited his sturdy cabin, two miles' walk from town in a stand of mixed hardwoods too close in to have caught the interest of the lumber company. It was in this structure that Gaspar painted when he did not paint outside, here that he stored most and displayed a few of his stacks of canvases painted with intense color (*saturated* was Gaspar's word for it) made by the unusually thick application of oil paint (*intaglio*, he called this technique). And it was here that he imparted what I considered then and consider again a certain amount of wisdom.

It was also here that one of the crucial moments of my life would pass—not unnoticed but, in the way of youth, underestimated.

But that was still some weeks away, and the afternoon I recall now was like so many others: Gaspar and I talking easily while I watched him paint.

"But you only paint trees and birds," I said. "You don't paint people."

He smiled. "Not often, but sometimes. That doesn't mean I don't think about them and try to figure out why they do the things they do."

"The laws of nature are easier to understand," I said, thinking about Nanette and then worrying that Gaspar was trying to tell me something I wasn't mature enough to understand.

✦ ✦ ✦

In the seventeenth century, the Italian engineer Guglielmini made observations of the Po River that led him to argue that alluvial rivers, without fail, carry the heaviest sediment load possible. The faster the current, he insisted, the more sediment a river does and indeed must carry.

Two centuries later, proponents of a levees-only policy for the Mississippi River argued with religious fervor—and not without attentive listeners—that levees not only block floodwaters but increase the velocity of water, causing the river to carry more sediment and thus to dredge its own bottom, deepening it and rendering it capable of carrying ever more water. The creation of outlets only undoes the genius of levees, they argued, and some went so far as to advocate the sealing off of even naturally occurring spillways.

Others voiced support for a more balanced policy of using outlets and cutoffs in combination with levees—of using all available means. Some of these engineers, all of them from private firms and not on the military corps payroll, cautioned that building ever-higher levees without the addition of outlets, regardless of any benefits gained in water speed, ultimately only deepened the river. Any more water the river channeled, some whispered, was more water the river could and eventually would spill across land.

✦ ✦ ✦

It took several weeks of negotiating, but my father finally granted Charles Segrist's request. He agreed that I could chauffeur on the conditions that I miss school rarely if at all, that I be paid, but not more than the going rate, and that my earnings go not into my pocket but into an account marked for college. I would have acquiesced to any stipulation that got me to New Orleans.

Before leaving to pick up Mr. Segrist for the first time, I put on my newest suit and promised my mother I would neither drink alcohol nor talk to women with short hair or short skirts. I had never seen such a creature outside magazine pictures and didn't have the slightest idea what I might have to say to one. So I made the promise in ignorance, already excited by the very words *woman* and *short*.

I had driven the car my grandfather had retired, and I had ridden in a few others, including Miss Fontenot's on a trip to a debate competition in Banville. But Charles Segrist's car was something else entirely, a different genus of thing: all leather and chrome and specially ordered and made. It was quieter, too, and smoother-riding than any vehicle I had ever sat in. Even on the cracked and narrow roads that wound their way through swamp and woods, toward what Mr. Segrist called civilization, the car was elegant.

For a long while, I was too frightened that I might drive the perfect car off the imperfect road to even acknowledge his attempts at conversation with more than a humming noise in my throat or a slight shrug of my shoulders. I flinched each time a tire hit a pothole or the smallest insect flattened in a smear against the windshield.

"According to Pliny," I ventured after the better part of an hour had passed, "it is universally accepted that the most advantageous time to fell timber trees is when the moon and sun are in conjunction."

Charles Segrist's burnished hair blew with the wind breezing through the open windows, and his smile was easy and wide. He wore a cream-colored suit, checked shirt, and red tie—a getup I'd seen him in when arriving from or heading for New Orleans but never when he planned both to wake and fall asleep in Cypress.

"Well, Louis, that is most interesting. But you'll have to agree with me that the best time to fell trees in Louisiana is when labor is cheapest or the price for lumber is highest. Preferably both at once."

I nodded. "I can't disagree with you, sir, though I guess the matter turns on the definition of *advantageous.*"

He brought out his polished laugh then. "I'll allow you that, Louis. But I'm guessing—and do correct me if I'm wrong—that your man Pliny did not have his money tied up in lumber."

I combed my mind for a clever retort but did nothing more impressive than watch the trees file by the window.

"You amuse me, Louis." He smiled more and shook his head as though I could not see him. "I plan to show you a thing or two. Or maybe even three. I think I am going to enjoy seeing my beloved Crescent City through your clever but—pardon me, I must say it—naive eyes."

✦ ✦ ✦

When the state government of Louisiana moved its capital to Baton Rouge in the 1840s, artisans were hired to make the cypress boards in the capitol look like oak, which was considered a more dignified and refined wood. These craftsmen spent long hours with narrow paintbrushes and dark paint as they sought to give the cypress the appearance of a grain it did not possess.

Eventually cypress would become a wood more prized than oak. Yet because it takes more than a century for each cypress tree to mature enough to produce good lumber, today cypress is mostly harvested young and sold as mulch.

✦ ✦ ✦

Within hours of arriving in New Orleans for the first time in my life, I found myself in one of the city's opulent clubs, eating oysters and several foods bearing names I had never heard and whose ingredients I could not discern.

The music, too, was unlike anything I knew. The musicians were white, but the music sounded closer to what I had heard coming through the door of the tunk in the Negro quarter the few times my father had invited me to accompany him on his Saturday-night rounds. Yet this music wasn't quite like that, either. It was busier, filled with more notes. One of the musicians played a clarinet, and the ensemble included no singer. Under the music tinkled the sounds of people eating and conversing. The dance floor near the stage was occupied by a few older couples and one young couple who leaned against each other.

Mr. Segrist insisted that I call him Charles, and I managed to comply about half the time, more often than not still calling him "Mr. Segrist" or "sir."

Though I kept part of my promise to my mother by sipping iced tea instead of champagne, I could not keep my full promise without being rude. The woman who joined us, the woman wrapped with great familiarity by Charles's arm, had hair sheared off at her chin and wore her dress hemmed shorter than any woman I had ever seen.

"The trombone player was in the Friar's Society Orchestra," she told me. "Some people called them the Rhythm Kings, so maybe you've heard of them that way—but he bugged out after they moved to Chicago. Said he didn't like the cold, said he couldn't stand to be away from New Orleans."

Her name was Mignonne. She was older than I was, of course, and more mature than the girls I knew. But somehow she was also more girlish than the women of Cypress, even than Miss Fontenot. Part of this was her height. I had practically a foot on her, and she seemed tiny next to Charles, whom she called Charlie. I thought she was like a Thumbelina, that she could almost dance on a man's hand. She was thinner, too, than the women I knew. In her dress without real sleeves, the shape of her arm bones was visible, as were her thin lines of muscle. And yet she occupied her small space fully—using sweeping gestures and laughing with her whole body—and the tautness of her skin made her seem more ample than she was. I couldn't look at her without flushing.

Charles took some fun with this, telling me to cover my lap with my napkin as though I wouldn't understand the joke. But Mignonne herself was kind, speaking to me only a little, about the music and the food. She asked no straight-on questions that would have made me reveal my ignorance. She searched with her dark eyes when she did speak to me, giving me one place I could look with what felt like relative safety, one place I could look without feeling the blush creep up my neck in red fingers.

Charles spoke of the difference between old and new money and how most Americans, though more out West than in New Orleans, don't care nearly so much about where your money came from as they do about how much you have. "But it is still in your best interest to act like you have old money. A lot of money is better than a little, but old money is never worse than new." Drinking his fourth glass of champagne, Charles lowered his voice to emphasize the word *never* and pulled it out long, almost slurring it. "The key is to be vague about where you got it. When people ask, I smile, wave my hand a little so they see my nice manicure, and say, 'Right now it's a little lumber, a little sugar.' Or better still, 'Wood,' I say, or 'Raw materials.' Most folks just peck around the question if they've got any breeding at all, and if they don't, then they do me little good anyway." He held the candle to his cigar and puffed it until it smoked in bursts like a steam engine.

When Mignonne rose to leave, using the term *powder room,* Charles ran his finger along her hem, seemingly for my benefit. I watched her walk away from the table, her steps in dainty time with the jazz coming from the stage.

Two men, both older and one considerably stouter than Charles, stopped by the table for a greeting. I was introduced as "my young friend, Louis Proby," and was flattered not to be identified as the chauffeur. The men were introduced by name, Hancock and Soileau, before they moved on to greet friends at another table.

Charles told me then that they sat on the boards of more than one of the city's most important and richest banks. "What's more," he went on, "it's supposed to be a secret, though it isn't much of one, that Hancock was Comus at Mardi Gras year before last. You know what the saying of Comus is?"

I shook my head.

"The saying of Comus is *Sic volo, sic iubeo.*"

I concentrated, but my French had only confused what little Latin I had encountered reading.

Charles smiled. "It's not important, Louis, because you can look up whatever you want to know. In this case, I'll simply tell you. *Sic volo, sic iubeo*: As I wish, so I command. Those two, I'll tell you." Charles shook his head and shifted his gaze toward the elaborate chandelier that sprinkled our table with blue and pink light. "They tolerate me because they know I might be one of them someday, maybe even someday soon. And if not, they will doubtless find some less noble use for me."

When Mignonne returned, Charles stood. As she passed him to take her seat in the booth, he swatted her, hard, on her bottom with his open hand. She laughed, not even in surprise, and my neck and face flushed all at once.

✦ ✦ ✦

By 1860, engineers with conflicting assumptions and competing visions already vied for control of the Mississippi. The wisest—as measured by the sometimes reliable test of time—were those whose understanding of the river was most direct, most intimate. These were the men who had swum the river, felt corporally the pull of its eddies and tows, descended its opaque depths in the earliest diving bells.

Most deltaic rivers have sandbars blocking their mouths. Only the Mississippi—due to the tremendous weight of new sediment it holds—generates mud lumps that lift from the water like startled animals, their cones spewing gas and wet mud and salt, leaving behind in minutes an island of several acres.

One of the brightest engineers to set his mind to the churning and dangerous puzzle of the Mississippi was a passenger on a boat lifted from its motion and slapped down on such an island, a piece of sudden land born in an instant. And so his knowledge of the river was not abstract. Yet the attitude of even this man toward the great and chaotic flow of water was characterized by arrogance.

"If my profession was not one of precise science," he stated, "then I might worry. But every current and turn of the river, indeed its every atom, is controlled by laws as fixed and certain as those which direct the heavenly spheres. Every eccentricity and trick of the river is directed by laws as immutable as the Creator, and the engineer needs only to ensure that he does not overlook the existence of any one of these laws to be certain that he will one day soon control the water. And if such is the case, he will rule its surface."

✦ ✦ ✦

In the days leading up to the Cypress festival, held each year to mark spring even if it already felt like summer, my father had been taking bets against his boasts about Terrebone's tenacity. "He'll make it to the top of the flagpole and down," he'd told every man who worked under him. Almost everyone in town except those few most deeply opposed to gambling had money on the event or planned to as soon as they had a little to put down.

Set for noon, the flagpole bet would unofficially open the Saturday afternoon of festivities sanctioned by the local women and sponsored by the lumber company in the form of a check signed by Charles Segrist, who would himself be celebrating the change of seasons in grander style elsewhere.

Shortly before noon, my father and I walked to the square with Terrebone trotting ahead. Pal stayed behind, crying in Luta's arms.

Luta, still wearing her uniform from the morning's triumphant basketball game against the Banville girls' team, shushed him. "Everyone knows that Terrebone has stronger jaws than most dogs three times his size and a more powerful sense of purpose than most people," she told him.

The central square was thickening with adults and children, horses and dogs. Men struggled with the awkward size of long tables, which they set end to end in rows—enough, it seemed, to seat the entire town. Women followed in short order with tablecloths and small vases of flowers and herb sprigs. Others carried platters and serving bowls and large covered roasting pans.

There were already a dozen or more pies set on one table. Behind that table stood Corinne Danger, paintbrush in hand, coloring in the sign announcing the pie-eating contest that Henri Lançon had vowed to win again and by a wide margin. "By any means necessary," he had announced at school.

One year earlier, at more or less the same moment, I had stalked the rows of tables scanning for watermelon pickles, preferably those that had been put up by Ann Washburn, who made the best. Now my eyes searched only for Nanette. But none of the Lançons was to be seen.

After greeting me, the doctor's wife returned to painting dark-blue letters on plywood with her left hand. I had noticed that Nanette, too, though compelled at school to hold her pen in her right hand, used her left for cutting with scissors or passing out papers. I wondered if left-handedness was more common among the French, though my empirical evidence was scant. Perhaps, I thought, I would gather my courage and ask Miss Fontenot if she naturally favored her left hand. *Gauche,* I thought, *sinister.*

The dentist passed the table of pies and lifted his white hat, distinctive in Cypress for its relatively narrow brim, which marked it as more fashion than protection.

My mother never said anything about anyone that was not pleasant or, at the least, generous in its effort to understand. But I had heard other women say to her that Corrine Danger put on airs, that she condescended, that she thought she was better than other people on account of her curly black hair and marriage to a doctor. My mother always changed the topic, but I sometimes wished that she would do more, that she would tell the women that Mrs. Danger was never anything if not polite.

Now, though, I saw that Mrs. Danger did not acknowledge the dentist's presence even after he tipped his hat. I noticed that she studiously avoided meeting his gaze despite the fact that she was his patient and the two attended the same church. The letter she was painting, the *t* in *today,* was wobbly and thin compared to the other letters in her sign. She dipped the brush in the glob of dark blue and traced over the letter, leaving it now noticeably thick and heavy. She stared at it for at least as long as I watched her, which was longer than I should have.

I again scanned the crowd for Nanette's face but gave up when I saw men gathering near the flagpole, where my father stood taking last-minute wagers, including one from Orlando Funes. I had to concentrate to register what I saw, struck as I was by its peculiarity.

I well knew that my father had little patience for those trappers who augmented their income with commodities of a different sort, particularly those who had been mixed up in the Cytrapper wars. And Funes himself rarely showed his face in Cypress. Yet there he stood on his short legs, in good pants but a work shirt, his black hair shining like satin in the sun, his jaw set in a jut that seemed to challenge the world to comment on his badly scarred skin.

I helped my father remove the flag and fold it into a triangle, handing it to Betsy Washburn, the only woman clustered close. Her name suited her in that her face always looked as though she had just scrubbed it hard with a coarse cloth. Her sister, Ann—known to be far too shy to stand among men and indeed unlikely to attend the festival at all after delivering her platter of watermelon pickles—had an almost ghostly white face, though her neck would redden in a pattern like the spots on a giraffe whenever she was spoken to.

"Good luck to the little fellow." Betsy smiled at me.

My father unwrapped a chicken liver and rubbed it on the dirty rope before tossing it to Terrebone, who snapped it midair and swallowed it whole.

"Bite," my father commanded, holding between his hands the length of rope rubbed with the chicken liver. Terrebone clamped down and allowed himself to be hoisted from the ground.

My father raised our terrier, working hand over hand, straining just slightly against the small weight. The spectators called out pieces of encouragement or discouragement, depending on where their money lay. Betsy Washburn, one fleshy arm pressing the flag to her body and the other akimbo, whistled through her teeth. "Just look at the little fellow," she said.

Those who had bet on Terrebone tried to follow their money with more, while those who had bet against him were already challenging the fairness of rubbing chicken liver on the rope. When Terrebone reached the pole's apex, the whole square hushed, and I realized just how wide his audience was. It included not just those gathered close but almost everyone at the festival. All I could hear was a small boy or girl calling out, "Look at that up there!" Those with their money on Terrebone began to clap, and my father started to ease the dog lower.

Then, fast as one beat, Terrebone fell. He just unclamped his jaw and went down like a dropped stone, his back down and legs up until he righted himself in a midair twist. His legs gave sideways on impact, and his small body made a thud. He uttered no sound. Betsy Washburn dropped the flag and covered her face with her hands, but everyone else was still and quiet for the longest of moments. It was like time stopping, and it's a feeling I remembered when I studied relativity.

At first, I waited for someone to do something, and then I realized I was the person who was supposed to act, that we were all waiting for me. I went to Terrebone, felt his stomach for breath. Finally my father dropped the now nearly weightless rope and stooped over us.

"He's alive," I said, wondering whether my father's uncharacteristic delay suggested guilt over hurting the dog or merely disbelief that he had been wrong.

Then the bickering started, with those betting on Terrebone arguing that the dog had made it to the top and their opponents saying that making it just to the top didn't count, that he was supposed to make it down again.

Before he handed the wad of collected money to Betsy Washburn to distribute to Orlando Funes and the others who had bet against Terrebone, my father spoke against his own financial interests: "The dog failed. If you bet on him, pay up." Then he turned to me and said, "Our doctor thinks his hands are too fine to fix up animals. Take him to Rabbit, son. Rabbit might be able to do something."

I carried the dog, which was breathing but felt unnaturally

heavy, south into the Negro quarter. On the near side, the houses were company-built—mostly smaller than the houses in Cypress proper. Some were whitewashed instead of painted but still were made from the same materials. Farther on, the houses became irregular, built from scrap and corrugated tin and tar paper. Streets gave way to uneven paths, and the dwellings, vegetable gardens, and clotheslines were oriented every which way.

A few people sat on porches in the cool afternoon, most of them women minding children playing in small packs. I knew that the sight of a tall white boy carrying a small, injured dog was not something they saw every day. A few waved, but most just watched me pass, their heads turning with my progress.

Rabbit answered the door to his house, which was assembled from assorted materials but larger and sturdier than most of the places on the southern edge of the quarter. He saw immediately what he was wanted for. "Bring it around back," he said.

The shaded yard, which smelled strongly but not unpleasantly of manure, was lined with pens and cages and corrals holding various half-tame and domestic animals, including hares, pheasants, hens, a small pig, two brown goats, a ewe and her lamb, a fawn, and some snakes tangled around a branch. Roaming free were several dogs and a dozen or more cats.

There in his backyard, under a light dappled by oak and pecan leaves, Rabbit examined Terrebone. Though his hands, if set side to side, were almost larger than the dog, he touched him with great gentleness. "This little dog is going to be fine, or I'm no veterinarian." Rabbit grinned and then laughed hard.

I stayed standing and close, my feet fidgeting with fallen pecans, while Rabbit worked on a table. As the dog started to rouse, I helped hold him down and did my best to soothe him while Rabbit finished setting and splinting three broken legs.

"You got to hurt to feel better," Rabbit said to the dog.

The quality of mercy to his work was its swiftness and the honeyed tone of his singing voice. His lullaby was soft and low: *"Gae, gae soulangae, baile chemin-la. M'a dit li, oui, m'a dit li, cowan li connais parle, ti cowan lis connais parle."*

"The little turtle knows how to talk," I translated in a whisper, recognizing only some of the Creole.

When Rabbit finished with his work, he instructed me to take Terrebone home, keep him inside and still, give him only water for the day but as much food as he would eat the next.

I paused, unsure about payment, but Rabbit told me: "It was when your father came to town that I realized that this was a place I might be able to stay, a place where maybe I could make something of my life. I'd hoped by now to have a son to pass along what I've learned, hoped maybe he could make a living at it without digging ditch, too. But I seem to be too ugly to get a woman to live here with me." Rabbit paused, then laughed. "But if my brother Ernest could marry, there's hope for anyone. Go on and take the little dog home. Your father will settle with me later."

By the time I carried Terrebone to the arms of my tearful sisters and brother and returned to the square, most of the town had finished eating. Amid the picked-over food I found a piece of chicken. Though the pink-and-white-flowered serving plate belonging to Ann Washburn was empty, I did find a few watermelon pickles that someone else had made.

The day before, I had all but decided not to enter the pie-eating contest on the grounds that I was too old and dignified. But the cards I had received from Miss Fontenot's class bristled. My classmates had remarked that, among such fine qualities as intelligence, lay arrogance and an unwillingness to dirty my hands. And so I told myself they were wrong, that I was not above sticking my face in pie filling, and that it was one way to get more than the single piece of pie most would have to settle for.

But now it was too late. In any case, no one seriously thought that anyone other than Henri Lançon would take first prize. With the rest of Cypress's young people and more than a few of its adults, I watched Henri devour pie. When the last of his competition retired, several of them sitting under trees rubbing their bellies and looking ill, Henri ate an extra half of a lemon meringue just for show.

When he finished, wearing a meringue mustache and luxuriating in the full attention of a large group, he entertained the crowd with a new stunt. Into each of his fingertips he stuck sewing needles—not thin basting pins pricked just under the skin like little boys will do, but real needles puncturing half an inch or more. He waved and fluttered his pierced fingers, grinning to the applause.

At last I sighted Nanette, lingering at the back of the crowd, leaning on and almost behind a large live oak. Her hair was down and ribbonless, and she bit lightly on her bottom lip as she watched her brother's antics.

The same sensations that always arrived when I saw her came again: my chest tightened, and my legs buzzed, almost numb. But I felt a surge of mental energy from my strange day, and the effect of Charles Segrist's confidence with Mignonne had not been lost on me.

I walked over to Nanette, stood what I considered to be a little too close to be polite, and said, "Go for a walk with me."

"All right," she said, following as I started away from the square and toward the woods.

After we had walked in silence for a time, she said, "You know I was glad when I heard that your little dog wasn't dead."

I said the only thing that made sense to me: "I'm sorry about what I wrote on the card."

She turned, genuine surprise showing in the lift of her long eyebrows. "Why? You were mostly nice, and you were right." She stalled, then touched my arm, looked straight at me. "I'm sorry I didn't write a card for you. I tried to, but I had too much to say on the one side and too little for the other."

✦ ✦ ✦

South of Cypress and Banville, which share a latitude, the parish becomes thoroughly rural. Before giving way to marsh, it could, in the 1920s, boast only two clusters of habitation—almost small towns but nameless. Italians lived in one, and there they grew vegetables and a variety of vine-grown sponge, hauling their produce to market in Grenada and New Orleans. They also fought the soggy ground to grow oranges, making from them pulpy juice, still orange wine, and a carbonated citrus wine they good-naturedly called champagne.

The other settlement was populated by Isleños, a smaller cluster of the same people who populated Delacroix Island. They spoke a Spanish not unlike that spoken on the Canary Islands in the eighteenth century. With the exception of a small primary school and tiny dry-goods market, their town was nothing but dwellings save the complex webs and mazes of string, crisscrossing whole acres, from which hung muskrat skins turning harder than wood in the sun.

Though it was not evidenced by how they lived from day to day—for the most part drinking only from mosquito-plagued cisterns and subsisting without electricity—some of these trappers grew rich by farming and skinning the rodents. The most successful made more in a season than the governor of the state was paid for a full year. And, naturally, many augmented their wealth off-season by rowing out to waiting ships, loading their boats with cases of whiskey and wine, and snaking their way toward New Orleans, where glasses always needed refilling.

Both Olivier Menard and Orlando Funes had come from this place. Funes still visited often with soda pop for the children, stockings for the women, and tobacco for his friends. He liked to tell the story of the day that Al Capone and his henchmen had visited, drinking and eating shrimp and home-cured olives with Funes in his cousin's home.

✦ ✦ ✦

Though evolution's millennia had hardwired me to recognize what was about to happen, I could not believe it. I could scarcely believe even what I could see: beautiful Nanette Lançon, dressed in the pale green of early spring, picking her way through the budding branches, now leading me as we walked out into the woods, away from the eyes and ears and talking mouths of Cypress.

Later I would try to reconstruct each sound, each rustle of clothing or leaf, each sigh or gasp, each kiss and touch and realization. I would strain to remember the precise order of events, the character of each sensation and wash of feeling. Yet the memory I took away was not a linear sequence but the burst of a moment, the entire afternoon like a mental flare.

Much later, when I gave concentrated attention to the idea of simultaneity, I would sometimes feel, even in a northeastern chill, the heat of that particular spring afternoon in a world now gone.

✦ ✦ ✦

Associated primarily with the tropics, leprosy has always been most prevalent in warm climes, including parts of Brazil, Nigeria, Madagascar, and Hawaii. In the continental United States, leprosy infection is limited to Louisiana and eastern Texas.

It is now known that this once mysterious disease is caused by *Mycobacterium lepra,* which thrives in hot geographical regions but in relatively cool regions of the body: the skin, the nerves just below the skin's surface, and the mucous membranes of the face.

Only a small percentage—perhaps one in twenty—of those infected with the bacterium ever develop leprosy. And those who develop the mild form of the disease suffer few ill effects beyond raised dark spots on their skin—no more alarming than an extreme beauty mark. Those who develop leprosy's more severe type and remain untreated, however, are gradually disfigured as their hands and feet grow ever more unsightly and their facial skin thickens in folds, sometimes claiming the very nose on their face.

✦ ✦ ✦

Less than two weeks after the spring festival, Terrebone began to move around the house, his three splinted legs clicking the floor like a waltz with an extra, silent beat. Luta and I encouraged his progress one Saturday morning, coaxing the dog across the living room with small pieces of leftover ground meat.

"No time for breakfast," my father told my mother as he came down the hall, tucking his shirt into his pants as he walked. "But you can make me a sandwich to take along. I've got seven crews to check on, and it's going to take all of the morning. Rabbit's group just about has the new skidder line in, but some of the other crews are working a whole lot slower than they could. Almost time to knock some heads."

I stood and brushed dog hair from the front of my pants.

"No," my father ordered. "You've fallen behind enough in your studies with all this driving to New Orleans business, not to mention your mysterious walks in the woods. You spend today cracking books."

He then told us that the doctor and his wife had announced they were moving to Lafayette, a city I had heard of but never been near, a city where Corinne Danger was known to have relatives.

"It's a real pity we can't keep a doctor in this town," my mother said from her work in the kitchen.

Dr. Danger had only two years earlier taken the place of the previous physician, who had left with his wife and son so that the son, who had been scrupulously schooled at home while they lived in Cypress, could attend a private secondary school in Baton Rouge.

Alone of Cypress's children, I had been invited to their home for carefully scheduled and supervised visits with the boy, James. James had been sickly looking—his mother believed that sun was deleterious to the intellect—but he was always glad of my company and possessed a wry sense of humor that made him affable. He also owned a stereoscope. Through it, I would gaze at three-dimensional pictures of the national parks. Each time I pictured myself, rucksack on my back, superimposed over the backgrounds.

"I want to see the world," I'd told James.

He'd nodded, somberly, and said, "Yes, I plan to also."

✦ ✦ ✦

In the *Praefatio* to his *Historia Naturalis,* Pliny the Elder—after dedicating the book, in groveling words, to Vespasian—modestly describes the project that follows as vacant of wit or clever oration. With somewhat greater hubris, he claims that "the nature of all things in the world, matters concerning our daily and ordinary life, are here deciphered and declared."

He goes on to attest to the simplicity of his language and the originality of his project's scope, noting the difficulty required to make old things new, to polish and invigorate that which is worn and out of use. It is hard, he argues, "to set a gloss and luster upon that which is dim and dark" and equally difficult "to reduce nature to all, and all to their own nature."

Pliny next praises—and appears quite willing to claim a spot among their ranks—those learned men and students who have "preferred the profit of posterity before the tickling and pleasure of itching ears in these days."

✦ ✦ ✦

Nanette held my hand as our feet sought the ovals of firm ground rounded up like turtlebacks from the half-land, half-water through which we made our careful steps. I was afraid that if I squeezed her soft hand too hard, it would disappear, with the rest of her, and I would find myself waking in a bed of harsh morning sun. I feared that if I held it too lightly, it would slip from my grasp and make her believe that my desire to touch her was insufficiently fervent.

"I know you don't like to look at their skins, but I thought, maybe because of that, you would care to see the signs of their living," I said.

First I showed her the raft of cattail stalks, cut into neat lengths and bound with grasses. "They rest while they eat," I explained, "so they make these."

Next I led her onto wider but soggier ground and pointed to the matted sheets of marsh grasses formed by the stout rodents into homes. "Muskrats have different houses for eating than for the rest of living. Their real houses have many chambers. One is for nesting. But this here is just a rest house, so it has only the one room."

"And this," I continued since she didn't seem bored, "is a scent post." I gestured toward the mat patched together with sedge leaves and mud. "They have scent glands, and they leave their smell for other muskrats."

"Why do they do that?" Nanette asked, her voice a little husky.

I thought I had once known the answer and tried to extract it from my memory. It came to me, but too late, and I said nothing but only shrugged. I was relieved when she laughed and slipped her hand inside my elbow.

✦ ✦ ✦

In charge of the regional weather bureau office in New Orleans was an esteemed meteorologist named Isaiah Clarke. Throughout the early spring of 1927, sometimes against the admonitions of his superiors in the nation's capital, he repeatedly raised his already high estimates of the expected flood stage at the Carrolton Street marker. In early April, he began to issue flood bulletins.

The newspapers in New Orleans, some of which held dramatically different political but remarkably similar economic aims, did not publish or even mention Clarke's bulletins.

While the meteorologist agreed with the opinions of most independent engineers and the wishful thinking of the New Orleans elite that the city itself was not in danger, he grew infuriated at the stubborn self-interest of the papers read by those in charge of many outlying areas that were, he was sure, in the gravest of danger.

Finally a single paper did report rising water and advised the usual precautions against flood, but not one New Orleans banker or businessman or editor had any real interest in suggesting that a penny of capital was in the least peril in their fine city.

Clarke knew deep water personally. He had survived the Galveston hurricane of 1900, pulling his two daughters onto the roof of their home, which proved an accidental raft they were able to ride ashore. He had not, however, been able to grasp the hand of his wife, who was never seen again.

✦ ✦ ✦

"It's just a spot of trouble, nothing new." My father's voice was gruff.

My mother smiled, yet her chin lifted higher than usual, higher than looked comfortable, and it tightened the skin of her face. The crescents under her eyes wore shadows.

I cleared my throat so that they would hear me coming, wouldn't think that I'd been eavesdropping. "Pal and Emily are asleep," I said. "And Luta's either still reading or she fell asleep with her lamp on."

I hoped my parents might, as they rarely but sometimes did, invite me to sit up with them and listen to the phonograph. But my mother merely thanked me for my report.

"I suppose I'll go read myself to sleep, too." I kissed my mother's cheek, nodded to my father.

There was no place to linger and listen without their noticing, so I had no choice but to retire to my room for the night. I felt too awake to read myself tired, so I pulled out one of my notebooks and worked on my entry for the bald cypress.

Taxodium distichum, I wrote at the top of the notebook page. On a piece of scrap paper, I jotted down, in the order of memory, everything I knew about the bald cypress from seeing or hearing or reading.

The tree was a relative of the giant redwood found in California, I knew, and could live for several thousand years. From my school course in Louisiana geography, I knew that it was economically important, used as it was in railroad and housing construction. I knew from my own knife cuts that the soft, pale wood was papery instead of grained and that the brown bark was smooth but fibrous. It was not a true cypress but, as a distant cousin, neither wholly other. Cranes and some songbirds were fond of its seeds. The bald cypress was a swamp-grower that dropped its needles in winter. In deep winter, cypress knees grew up from its ridged base, poking up through the water's surface, toward air.

I stared at my list of facts, wondering how I might organize them by kind and rank them by importance. I knew, too, that they were facts and only facts; they did not add up to the species I wanted to describe.

The most important thing I had written, I understood, was that the bald cypress could live three thousand years. My young mind worked to fathom what one tree might have lived through, a single century at a time—how many generations of birds, much less insects, it had felt come and go. Yet after a while, it seemed that this line of thinking was taking me even further from capturing the bald cypress's essence in a way I could set to paper.

Recalling Gaspar's comments on the river, I tried to think about it in another way. First I concentrated on why the cypress knees grew as they did, what purpose they served. The unusual feature was, surely, the most telling. Perhaps the odd protrusions drew more sun or air to the water-bound tree, served the creature they seemed so intent on growing away from.

Next I tried to think as the painter might. I closed my eyes, conjured a single bald cypress from a stand of them, attempted a mental sketch, first of its needles, then of its general form.

There was something human in its shape, something dignified but deeply sad.

When I opened my eyes, I felt silly thinking how meaningless it is to attribute to nonhuman things the characteristics of people.

And so I stayed up late into the night and then slept thickly, waking only with difficulty and only when the daylight in my room was full. Smelling coffee but not breakfast, I dressed hurriedly.

Only Luta was in the kitchen. Her shoulders collapsed, her arms on the table, her forehead resting heavily on the back of her hands, she sobbed so hard that her back convulsed.

"What has happened?" I asked. "What's wrong?"

She looked up, her face swollen and smeared with the blush of crying. "Someone killed Buck. Someone killed Buck and threw a rock through the window with a note saying that Daddy's next."

Something inside me straightened. "Where is he?"

"Dead in the yard!" Luta sobbed with renewed vigor.

I pressed my hand on her back, feeling it fill with air and then empty with a shudder. "I'll take care of Buck. I'll bury him," I said. "But tell me where Daddy is."

"He and Mama took Emily and Pal to the new house. Daddy says we're all to move in there now, because it's farther back and higher up from the street and all."

Suddenly in control of her crying, Luta lifted her head and sat erect. "I guess we'll never sleep in this house again." Her statement sounded neutral, neither happy nor sad, more fact than feeling. "Oh, there's coffee on the stove. Daddy said you were to have a little and then take me over to the new house."

I poured the coffee, which was viscous and syrupy from sitting too long on the heat.

"I'm scared, Louis. Don't leave me alone." Luta fixed her light eyes on me and tried to smile a little.

A few days later, I was boxing my mother's kitchen implements for hired men to carry to the new house. I heard my father's boots, louder than usual in the almost empty rooms, and looked up to find him filling the door frame between what had been our kitchen and living room.

"I need you to come with me to Grenada," he said, his voice flat.

"Today?" I asked.

"As soon as you can get yourself cleaned up."

As we drove through slanted rain, the tires whirring on the wet road, I wanted to break the silence. I wanted to ask my father what was happening but could not. I wanted at least to talk about what seemed the most important hours of my young life—my time alone with Nanette—but I couldn't raise that subject either. I could, however, approach it by talking about the day on which it had happened.

"Henri Lançon won the pie-eating contest again," I said. "I suppose everyone knew he would."

My father held his head halfway through the side window,

despite the rain. His hair blew wildly, flinging droplets of water across the front seat. I didn't expect him to answer, but he did: "That so?" And then, "What's your estimation of the Lançon boy? There's two kinds of clowns. Would you say he's the smart kind or a stupid one?"

Unsure, I paused.

"What I'm wondering," continued my father, "is whether the company might have some use of him. Some positions need to be filled by a fellow who's going to be outgoing and friendly, only not stupid about it. And he speaks local and French both, right?"

I couldn't remember my father soliciting such an opinion from me before, and I considered my words before I delivered them. "I used to think he was a smart fellow, just one that needed attention bad enough not to care how." I began haltingly and gained confidence. "But now I wonder about that, because after the pie-eating contest Henri was walking around the square with pins stuck in the ends of his fingers, waving them at everyone."

My father's head jerked toward me, and cool drops of water hit my forehead and cheek.

"What do you mean by 'pins stuck in the ends of his fingers'?"

I told him about the sewing needles shining out like those long fingernails on the old holy man from India in the Ripley cartoon. "It was like he didn't even feel it," I added.

My father fell silent again, his attention divided between his side of the windshield and his still-open window. I watched the wet road move under us and wished he had allowed me to drive.

He drove too fast around slick curves but unnecessarily slow on the straightaways.

"I've thought about the pros and cons of it," my father said, giving me just a moment to realize that he had changed subjects and was no longer talking about Henri Lançon. "You're going to have to come inside with me. I don't want you to look around at anything you don't have to look at. Don't say much in there, and afterward don't repeat anything. And don't ask me any questions I don't want to answer."

I nodded, but my father wanted more. "Got that straight? That all clear?" he demanded.

"Yes, sir. I understand what you are saying to me."

My memories of Grenada, the parish's largest town and, not coincidentally, the one closest to New Orleans, were not fond. I had been there only twice, both times waiting for my father to transact business about which I knew nothing and could not ask.

Aside from the smell of the place, which had kept my stomach unbalanced for the whole day, I held a single memory of the first visit, when I must have been about six or seven. Grenada's streets, all made of shell crushed and fused into a hard surface, sprawled between open drainage ditches. Bored with waiting and driven to the water the way children sometimes are, I had shed my shoes, rolled up my trouser legs, and waded into the canal that followed the eastern edge of the main street.

Within only minutes, something tightened around my ankle, something I could not kick free. I made my way back toward the dry embankment with the large, slow steps that water requires, working my pocketknife loose from my belt as I pushed forward, preparing to cut myself loose from whatever length of rope or twine had me by the leg.

Once above the waterline, standing on the steep slope of the ditch, I stared, mouth agape, at the large eel spiraled tight around my lower leg. I felt its muscled body, squeezing, and tasted the retch of my stomach bile. Not until two passing men began to laugh at me did I realize that I was screaming.

By the time my father emerged from a storefront, I had peeled the eel from my leg and was puncturing points of the flailing body with my boy's knife. But I guess I was still screaming.

My father bracketed my shoulders from behind. "All right, son. You're done of it now."

On my second trip to Grenada, I better understood the nature of the sickening smell that pushed through the town as a slow but ungentle breeze. Permeating the air, saturating it, was the smell of rot and blood and decomposing hide that filled the abattoirs that gave work to hundreds of parish men.

Yet the smell was not so simple as death because the largest single operation in Grenada was a sugar refinery—the world's biggest at the time. And so it was that, wrapped up in the odor of slaughter, was the sweet smell of sugar in each of its states from cut cane to the sparkling white crystals that fill a sugar bowl.

Because of the memory of the choking eel and the horrible mixing of sweetness and death, I had not been anxious to return to Grenada. And for years I was in luck because my father was no more anxious to bring me as an older boy than I was to go. But his disincentive was different: the casinos and the liquor sold in them as freely as if the selling of liquor were legal. Grenada was home to several of these casinos, including the Moorish Club owned by Olivier Menard.

Menard may have been the tallest man in Cypress Parish, literally as well as figuratively. Based on the few times I had seen him, I guessed that he might even have measured closer to seven feet than six. His skin was pocked and scarred, yet despite that and despite his outsized stance, his appearance was refined. His black hair was, in middle age, thick and shiny. His mustache and beard were likewise silky and closely groomed. His eyes, though set too close to the high bridge of his straight nose, had a clearness that suggested intelligence. His mouth was thick, but not lewdly so.

Like his rival Orlando Funes, Menard had been born into an Isleño trapping family. But his family had been better educated than the one that had reared Funes. Menard's mother spoke French as well as her Isleño Spanish, and she had her son read Balzac and Flaubert even as he learned to raise and skin muskrat. Like Funes, he was better at trapping than his father and grandfather had been—and in a more auspicious economy. And like Funes, Menard had to credit his eventual affluence more to liquor and gambling than to the sale of muskrat skins.

And affluent he was. The Dorsey Brothers as well as the most famous Negro jazz bands from St. Louis and even Chicago played at his club, which gave away a new car every week of the year. And Menard's son, having just completed medical school at Tulane, was furthering his studies in Paris, where Menard himself was said to travel twice a year in order to indulge his expensive tastes in food.

When my father had told my mother about Menard's son, she had been alarmed, worried that a stretch of decadent European life might follow my medical studies.

"Louis can go straight into practice," my father had told her, smiling at her relief.

Though Menard trafficked in the roughest of liquors, his own basement was rumored to be stocked with good wine and vintage port. Unlike the French heard through much of Cypress Parish, Menard's was ruled by Parisian grammar and marred by no inelegant inflection. It was said that he still read, that he considered his library his most valuable possession. It was known that his deceased wife had been European born and well born—even very well born, if Betsy Washburn's hints about a count's daughter held any truth.

But there was nothing aristocratic about the empire Menard had created. It was a kingdom of lowly and mostly illegal activities, a kingdom built on human weakness, or at least self-indulgence. This made it, if anything, more rather than less of an empire in the world of its time.

It was midmorning when we parked the car and walked toward the Moorish Club. Only a few people walked about, and no one sat on the stone benches that lined the storefronts of Grenada. I heard the crunch of my boots, and my father's, on the crushed-shell road. The rain had subsided, leaving it hotter and more humid as steam rose from the ground and the sun emerged. I tried to but could not ignore the mixed odors of blood and sugar that flared my nostrils. To give myself moments of relief, I tried breathing through my hand or the sleeve of my shirt, but there was no avoiding the stench. I wondered how anyone could live in the town and supposed people could get used to anything.

There were more people in the casino than walking about the town. A few stood and talked at the bar, but most were scattered around at card tables. The stage was empty except for a young man sweeping, and it was dark except for a single spotlight. The stale smell of the previous night's liquor and cigars soaked the unmoving air, and the floor was littered by matchsticks, cigarette butts, losing raffle tickets, and paper napkins, some bearing names and addresses that had been cast aside.

Menard was expecting us, the hostess said. The woman had an ugly face, but she looked good in her tight yellow dress, and I watched her as I followed her to the stairs at the back of the building, realizing that I saw women differently now that I had seen and touched one undressed.

I was expecting some scene out of a Western, but we found Menard seated at a gleaming cherrywood desk in a large, book-lined office. He was alone and working figures in a ledger with a sharp cedar pencil.

He stood when we entered, invited us to chairs with a flourish of his large hand. "Coffee?" he asked.

"We're not here for refreshments," my father said, and I was embarrassed by his incivility.

"Or course not. I understand." Menard resettled himself in his chair, clasping his hands before him on the desk with what struck me as great frankness. "Let's proceed with our business, then. I understand you are having trouble with my old acquaintance."

I surveyed the shelves of books that lined, floor to ceiling, the walls surrounding Menard's desk. I read the titles of anatomy and chemistry texts, of English and French novels, of European histories. Menard turned to follow my gaze and then returned to my face. Heat rose in my neck, although I knew that Menard's look of curiosity—almost bemusement—was only natural. It was as peculiar a thing for a country boy to be absorbed by books at such a moment as it was for a man in Menard's profession to house such a library.

"I don't mind the trouble for myself, but Funes has threatened my home. He has come near my family." My father sat stiff, hands on his knees as he leaned slightly forward on his straight arms, ready to stand in an instant.

"You may recall our earlier conversation—some years ago now, was it not?" Menard sat back now, crossed his legs, moving his folded hands to his lap.

"If you can take care of Funes for me, I can assure you that your men—"

"My employees?" Menard smiled, lifted his eyebrows just a bit into his high forehead.

"Fine, then," my father said. "I can assure you that your employees will not be stopped in Cypress or its environs."

"Then we have only to shake hands to call ourselves friends."

My father waited for Menard to stand first before rising to shake the tall man's hand. Then my father motioned to me with his left hand in a way that told me I was to remain seated, that I was not to shake Menard's hand. I understood that my father had compromised himself and did not want me compromised any more than I already was by virtue of being in the room.

"Of course there may be other little things from time to time as well, but that's nothing but *lagniappe* between friends." Menard tipped his chin slightly toward me. "If I was a betting man—which of course would be unwise in my position—I'd say your boy likes books."

My father pressed his hands to his side, nodded just perceptibly. "Louis will be a doctor."

In my relatively limited experience in automobiles, I had noticed that the drive home from anywhere usually seemed shorter than the drive there. But that wasn't the case on the drive home from Grenada, in the once again heavy rain. By the time we were at last close to Cypress, my father had said nothing about the meeting with Menard save one sentence: "It is my plan for you that you never have to do anything like that."

There were questions I wanted to ask, but I could not, and anyway I had a sinking certainty that I already knew the answers. I let my head lean against the window, my eyes close. I invoked Nanette's soft skin and the sound of her whisper near my ear. I thought about the next time I would see her alone, feeling the blood pulse through my veins in the syncopated beat of my heart.

✦ ✦ ✦

Often the history we might learn from is long forgotten. Other times, the past is so recent that we learn the wrong lesson.

In 1927, people could well remember 1922, and nowhere better than in New Orleans. Though engineers trumpeted aspects of the 1922 flood as evidence that the Mississippi River would soon be confined, seventy thousand people—many of them in Cypress and neighboring parishes—had been left homeless that year.

Waves had splashed over the tops of levees in New Orleans, where almost half a million people lived with no means of evacuation. While newspapers and city officials declared the city safe, in the already world-famous French Quarter sand boils erupted more than three hundred feet from the levee, shattering cobblestones and spewing small volcanoes of muddy water.

Then, some miles south of the city, a levee responsible for holding one of the river's sharp bends and taking the brunt of its current gave way. This crevasse opened a scant five miles from an inlet of the Gulf of Mexico and in the precise position of an artificial spillway that had been proposed but—under the influence of those advocating a levees-only policy—never constructed.

Though the 1922 crevasse took little human life, it forged a wall of water fifteen hundred feet wide and more than one hundred feet high—a wall of water higher than any building in New Orleans at that time. Much of two southern parishes was flooded, while in the city the river fell swiftly.

The Mississippi River Commission stated that the newly homeless had been victims either of backwater flooding or of substandard levees. The solution it hit upon was to bring all levees into line with the latest government specifications. As for backwater flooding: it was not wholly avoidable, and modern practicality would certainly have to include solid evacuation plans for rural people.

Meanwhile, some of the country's brightest but not necessarily most vocal engineers took away another lesson: human activities, including the closure of some of the river's natural outlets, were making the river more dangerous, particularly to Mississippi and Louisiana, at a time when more people than ever were living in its reach. "Our arrogance is making us vulnerable," one said.

Those who ruled New Orleans—and no one more than those who ruled with the practical power of money rather than the weaker authority of office—drew another conclusion altogether. The way they saw it, their city and its expanding wealth had been saved by a levee break to the south. More than one powerful man smiled at the thought that there now existed a last resort.

Once imagined, a last resort becomes not only possible but increasingly likely. Once imagined, it is a contingency that can be planned around. It can even be planned for.

✦ ✦ ✦

PART TWO

CREST

liny the Elder set out in late August of the year 79 to make detailed notes on the erupting Vesuvius. As his boat drew near to the beach at Pompeii, airy gray ash powdered the vessel's deck, powdered the hair and clothing of his entourage. A slave's hand was burned by a fragment of volcanic rock, and the man wore the numb pebble of flesh into his eventual freedom and then to his death.

Pliny was by no means easily resigned to his impotence, to his inability to reach land, though finally he realized that he was too late to assist the wife of a friend, a woman certainly already buried with the rest of the town. He ordered the boat south. Making their precarious way through now severe sea, the crew docked the boat at the harbor at Stabiae.

The old man rested on a sheet stretched taut on the beach against the wind. When he tried to stand, Pliny succumbed to the poisonous gases that fumed from Vesuvius and died in the arms of two long-held slaves. Though forced to flee then for their own lives, several members of his traveling party returned a few days later to recover his body.

In his well-kept and thick-walled home, in addition to the manuscript of the *Historia Naturalis,* Pliny left another one hundred sixty volumes of notes on the details of his world, including a significant number concentrating on the affairs of men. These, however, are lost to us; the *Historia Naturalis* is Pliny's only surviving full work.

As an older man, a busy man—a man with a brain full of complex ideas and large numbers—I thought little of this story. But on the verge of manhood, it preoccupied me. I thought that to die at such work, particularly at a venerable age, was at least a kind of heroism.

And often, as I stood and watched the people of Cypress moving noisily in the central square or coming in and out of shops, I imagined them frozen just as they were, in motion but asphyxiated, choked by the gas of a nonexistent volcano, buried in action like the citizens of Pompeii.

It took me a stretch of dream to realize that my father was shaking me from sleep. "Get cleaned up and dressed. You need to drive the dentist."

I threw off the sheet and stood, feeling as though I were still in my dream.

"Dress well. After you take him to the Moorish Club, you're

taking Segrist's car back to New Orleans. But you need to hurry. There's going to be trouble if we don't get him out of here fast."

My mind stumbled over my father's words, but I located and stepped into my pants, worked my arms into the sleeves of a dress shirt.

"Some of the men are already scrounging up feathers, and they're talking about making the tar extra hot. Part of me wants to let them, but that kind of trouble is no good in the long run. They might go all the way and string him up. Anyway, Menard wants him protected. Turns out he's his half-brother or first cousin or something."

When I emerged—face washed but unshaven, my tie around my neck but not properly knotted—Dr. B was already sitting in Charles Segrist's car. What little sky showed was dusted with stars, and I realized that the hour was as it felt: the middle of the night. Not until we were several miles from town did I register that it was, technically, my birthday.

After a time, I said to Dr. B, "You told me you were from South America. You told me stories about Santiago, how the buildings look. About the woman who sings so beautifully."

He fingered the narrow brim of the hat on his lap. "I guess I wished I was. But I'm just some Isleño who got himself a profession. What's great about this country is that I almost made the lie true. What's terrible about it is that I didn't get away with it, in the end. All because I fell in love."

"Is love why they're back there aiming to tar and feather you?"

He looked small as he nodded. "They think I am some hot-blooded Latin womanizer, but it's not true. My heart belongs to one woman. I never touched any of the others, even the ones who seemed to get an invisible toothache every week and batted their eyes in my chair. I never touched one of them, never even wanted to. I love one woman."

I nodded, and we rode on in the near silence of the tires turning over the road, the wind whooshing quietly by the car, the low insect hum of the wider landscape.

After a while, unprompted, he said, "It's true what I told you, you know, about the buildings. I've seen pictures."

Menard met us at the door to his club. "Thank you, Louis," he said, shaking my hand formally and meeting my eyes as though I were an adult. "Wait here a moment."

I stood on the plank porch that lifted the Moorish Club from the crushed-shell road. The smell of sugar refining was heavy in the air, but the blood smell was muted, covered in part by the smell of rotting fish and the fresher smell of impending rain. I realized that I knew the initial but not the name of the man next to me: a lovesick Isleño dentist standing there quiet and stoop-shouldered, still fingering the hat that usually covered his hair, which I noticed for the first time was beginning to thin.

"Of course you owe me nothing and do not even really know me," he said. "But Olivier will turn me down, and I have no one else to ask. So I have to ask you. I have written a letter. Please give it for me to Corinne."

"Corinne?"

Even as I inflected her name I understood why the doctor and his wife were leaving Cypress, why she had cried on her way through the dentist's anteroom, why her greeting at the spring festival had been so awkward. I began to understand, too, that people in love act differently than I'd imagined, that love wasn't the simple, happy thing that I wanted it to be, that I hoped it would be for Nanette and me.

Menard returned. He handed the dentist a thick envelope, saying, "Take a train somewhere and stay there for at least a month, and better forever. Better forever, but if you come back, come here or go to Delacroix. I have given my word that you are finished with Cypress, and I can't ensure your safety if you're unintelligent enough to go to Lafayette."

He handed me a book, saying nothing. I treasured the small, rectangular heft of the volume before turning it sideways so that I could read its spine. It was Darwin's *Voyage of the Beagle,* a book I had never before seen.

I looked at Menard, thanked him.

"It is not a debt," he replied. "It is just something because I thought you would like it and should read it. Maybe you'll get more from it than I had a chance to."

"Not a debt," I repeated, thinking of it as my first birthday gift.

I turned and headed for the car, knowing the dentist would follow.

In front of the train station, I wished him good luck. "I hope you can get a seat. Seems as though a lot of people are leaving ahead of the water."

He nodded. "And more will leave soon enough." He reached over the seat for his small suitcase and placed his hat on his head. "It is true what I told you about the buildings in Santiago. I've seen pictures."

"What about the woman who sings more beautifully than anyone on the radio?"

"She's real," he said, smiling. "There's a woman like that in every place."

The address I had been given proved to be a flat not far off St. Charles. "A good address," I imagined Charles saying, "is of greater importance than spacious accommodations."

It was too early to ring the bell without annoying him, so I set about disposing of an hour in the city that now seemed knowable, a place I could make my own if that was what I decided to do with my future. It was one of many options I planned to consider, the night's events and the date on the calendar making me feel older, more man than boy.

Even in the still-gray quiet of the new day, I heard more of the sounds of life's busyness than could be heard in Cypress at high noon. The sound of horseshoes clicking against rock, the motors and horns of the cars, strings of English and French and Spanish and a language I could not identify, the squeaky wheels of pushed carts carrying vegetables and sewing goods, the yawks of newspaper boys.

With my fingers, I counted the coins in my pocket and decided to read the headlines without purchasing a paper. There had been a murder in Gretna, I saw, of one business partner by another. Huey Long—the man people said would challenge the governor in the next election and who was a Protestant from up North—had made a speech. The results of boxing matches were posted, and the ladies' paper carried the usual housekeeping advice columns and reports of society parties. There was no mention of flood, or even of rainy weather.

A man next to me, a man who was my father's age and wore the white coveralls of a workman, snorted. "We don't need them to tell us what we can see for ourselves. Anybody would do better to walk to the levee at Carrolton than to read any of those papers."

At the breakfast counter where I ordered coffee with milk and an egg with grits, the talk was also of the relentless rains and the rising water.

"There's still more rain everywhere north," said a small, middle-aged man hunched over a bowl and trying to open a miniature box of packaged cereal. "They're nothing up there if not wet and soggy, and all that water's got no way to come except this way."

"They're organizing work camps in Mississippi," said the younger man cooking our food. "They know what's coming."

"They'll be readier than we will down here," the small man answered, and the cook agreed.

✦ ✦ ✦

During most of the spring of 1927, every major paper in the eastern half of the United States—as well as most papers out West and many in the capitals of Europe—carried on the very front page, nearly every day, news of the swelling tributaries, of the houses ruined, of the lost crops, of the record-battering rainfall, of the rising crests in the Mississippi itself.

No paper in New Orleans carried the weather or the swelling river on its front page. Occasionally, on page two or four or further back, news of the water-made homeless in states where most people in Louisiana had never been were given an inch or two of column space. From time to time, prominent placement was given to a favorable prediction that the river would, most assuredly, not threaten the Crescent City. But the editors of all the city's papers, together with the bankers who whispered in their ears, understood that to refute something too often is to lend it credence. They were mindful to mention even the most favorable forecasts only after considering carefully the timing and spacing of such reports. Less optimistic versions of the future were, needless to say, not printed at all.

✦ ✦ ✦

Mignonne's small feet made no sound on the tiled floor. As she turned and reached and made her way around the kitchen, preparing coffee and Charles's breakfast, I watched the ways that her robe moved or did not move with her body.

The robe was cinched tightly at the waist and had wide, flowing arms and a long skirt. At first the black-and-white pattern of its fabric looked random, the flowers and leaves and swaths of dots haphazard. But when I squinted slightly or held my eyes so still that my vision filmed, the material represented the night sky as seen by someone lying on his back in a garden, gazing through a tangle of flowered vines at the wide-open Milky Way.

I would retain and fine-tune this ability to shift my vision, and it would enable me, in my later life of science, to see connections where others saw only chance juxtaposition without meaning.

Charles, looking up from his magazine, called across me to Mignonne, "It seems that you have an admirer, *chérie.*"

Mignonne was kind enough to ignore the remark.

"Today is my birthday," I said, for no reason that I could understand, except perhaps to change the topic of conversation.

"That's brilliant news!" Charles slapped his leg with his magazine and nearly shouted. "We were almost without anything to celebrate today. A huge relief, Louis. I don't know what we would have done without you. You do us a great service, and you shall be rewarded decadently."

Mignonne winked at me, and I returned her small smile without blushing.

While Mignonne was out, Charles made more coffee, and as we drank it, he asked me about religion.

"I go to my parents' church on Sundays. It's the sort of church we've always gone to, the sort I was baptized in."

"Is that pretty much the end of it for you, then?" Charles organized his tobacco case while we talked—knocking used cut leaves from the bowl of a pipe and then cleaning the stem with a pipe cleaner, rolling cigarettes, trimming cigars.

"We don't study the Bible at home, if that's what you mean."

Charles laughed. "I didn't take your father for the hearth-side New Testament type, though of course it's better if you don't mention to him that Mignonne sleeps here. But I'm getting at something else. Religion *is* important."

This surprised me—the notion that Charles might have a pious side despite breaking all the rules I associated with piety. "Yes, sir," I said. "Of course it is."

He laughed, swished coffee around his mouth, lit a cigar. "No, Louis, I meant that religion is important socially. What I'm getting after is this: Are your convictions specific?"

I shrugged, considering the word *conviction,* then pointed at his tobacco case. "About as specific as your smoking habits. You seem to be prepared for anything there."

"That's good news, Louis. If you plan to go far—and I think and I certainly hope that you do—you're going to need to change churches. Down here, Catholicism is just dandy, but the process of converting would take up some of your time, and you'd have to be creative to get through it. Presbyterian could be all right, but Episcopalian is the safest and most portable. It's even fine for New Orleans unless you marry a rich Catholic girl, and there's nothing wrong with marrying a rich Catholic girl. But everything else but Episcopalian and Catholic is looked down on here. And even if you're a Papist, you don't want to go to church with too many Italians or Spaniards, and you don't want to be the sort that shows up for daily mass with the candle-lighting widows. Nope, you've got to be the sort of Catholic who writes handsome checks to both your parish priest and the diocese and attends mass exactly one Sunday out of three plus every holy day save a few." He puffed at his cigar and shook his head. "And of course it goes without saying: up front Christmas Eve, always at midnight mass, plus midday Easter Sunday. But really, Episcopalian's easier—and safest if you want to move north."

"You've given that a lot of thought," I said. "I suppose Baptist is no good?"

"I know your family's Baptist, but we're talking about your future. Hell, in New Orleans we've got fine Jews on most of the bank boards, though you won't find them at the club we went to last time or the one we're going to tonight—and you won't find them in the good Mardi Gras krewes. But in the best restaurants and in the boardrooms, at fine parties and in meetings where decisions are made, you'll find at least a few Jews. But not a single Baptist, Louis, so take note of that. No one wants some Baptist staring at him when he's trying to have a good time."

"What does it matter?" I had finished my coffee and held the empty cup and saucer on my knee, not sure where to set it.

"Men like you and me write our own future. You can come from anywhere in this country; you can even say you're from somewhere else if you fix how you talk. If you plan to stay in this great state, convert to the Catholics. Just say what they tell you—the sooner, the better. Otherwise go for Episcopalian. It will help you marry the right woman, and that's important. Most important, maybe, though the two go hand in hand."

"A woman like Mignonne?"

My question brought forth a strange laugh from Charles, who seemed both bemused and rueful. "No, Louis, pay attention. Mignonne is precisely the sort of girl you do not marry." After a stretch of silence, he added, "It's a sad but true fact that I'll soon have to trade in Mignonne for a woman I won't like half so well."

As if to cheer himself, Charles snubbed out his cigar, rose from his armchair, and said, "Let me show you how to dress. After all, there will probably come a time when that will matter most of all, assuming you've already got the God-given looks you and I are blessed with."

It wasn't until after my awe for Charles Segrist subsided—after I could identify his affectations and understand the degree to which he was a compromised person—that I could sort through his advice to take away some good untainted by the rest of it. I shared his ambition to rise in the world, but I knew soon enough what Olivier Menard knew: that dressing the part comes after being granted the role.

And yet, years later, I almost followed Charles's advice on religion, studying to become an Episcopalian. In the end, my fiancée married me even though I did not convert, and I dutifully escorted my wife to church most Sundays, standing there willingly but silently, never singing the hymns or even mouthing the words.

In reading about the history of the Christian church, I came across the story of St. Lawrence. It would be several generations after Pliny's death in the arms of his slaves before St. Lawrence would stand before one of Vespasian's successors to declare that the wealth of the Roman empire was to be found in its slaves, its beggars, and its lepers. For this statement, he was martyred by fire.

Some years later, the emperor who turned Lawrence to smoke was flayed alive by the Scythians, who saved and eventually returned his skin to the Romans.

With its marble foyer and faux-Roman statues and white-jacketed waiters, the club was even finer than the first one Charles had taken me to.

"It's the second best in town," he stated as though it were an agreed-upon fact. "Only the Louisiana Club is more elite, and you cannot bring a guest to it. When Theodore Roosevelt came to New Orleans in the middle of that yellow fever outbreak, I tell you he was a hero in this city. A god, even. Women were falling at his feet, and the most important men in town were falling over each other like fools to get a meeting with him. But even he couldn't get into the Louisiana Club for lunch until they made him a member. No outsiders allowed, not even presidents. But I'll tell you a secret, Louis: the food's much better here."

Wearing half-borrowed clothes but my own pants, I tasted the first champagne of my life. As I grew accustomed to its fizz and its clean, mineral taste, I listened to men possessed of wealth and its power discuss the future of the largest city I'd seen.

I thought at that moment that my life was beginning. *Seventeen,* I told myself, *is when it begins for me.* No longer fearing my birthday, I smiled, nodded to accept a refill, and forgave myself for the roughness of my hands against the elegant, tulip-curved flute. I assured myself—promised myself—that my hands would grow only softer and more pale. I would depart for college in a year, and my work from then forward would be indoors.

I remembered meeting Soileau before, at the other club, the night I had met Mignonne, though it struck me as odd that I had failed to note the missing arm. I wondered if I would have noticed it now had Charles not explained it in advance. Soileau, he said, had lost the arm when his new glass bathroom door had shattered. Immediately upon rehabilitation, he had used his powers of language and the nuances of Napoleonic law to extract a large sum of money from the company that had manufactured the door.

"The unforeseen perils of modern life and good taste in interior design," Charles had said drolly. Then he had spoken in a tone that carried more purpose: "Do not make the mistake of many, thinking that the loss of his arm has changed him in any way that is fundamental, in any way that matters. Soileau is neither softer nor meaner, not more compassionate nor less than before. He made a decision to be unchanged. He was shrewd when he had two arms, and he's shrewd today. Those who think the loss of the arm made him anything other than richer miss the point, so to speak."

I'd smirked at the dark pun but had not said what I was thinking, which was that I didn't see how the phantom presence of a limb that had once been used but was now gone could fail to change a man in some way. Soileau had, I assumed, punched an enemy with the fist of that arm and touched a woman with its fingertips.

I'd never really considered what the loss of a leg had done to my grandfather, except to his body and occupation. Perhaps now I was old enough to ask him about the intangible changes the loss had wrought.

Yet now, in Soileau's presence, I trusted Charles's opinion more fully. Charles and Soileau and the banker named Hancock and the two other well-suited men at the table argued over what to do about Isaiah Clarke's weather reports. Soileau was wiry, dark-headed, quick to speak, and sure in what he said. His handicap was evident only in the negative, only in his restraint in using strong gestures, which were, due to the force of his voice, all but unnecessary.

As the discussion heated, and under a look from Charles, Mignonne excused herself to greet acquaintances at another table. I waited for a similar direction, an unspoken suggestion that I dismiss myself from the table while weighty matters were discussed, but Charles instead drained the bottle of champagne into my glass before calling for another bottle to the waiter, who stood attentively near but not close enough to hear.

"Someone needs to pay off Clarke or step on him. Personally, I don't give a damn which approach we take." Hancock used his palm to smooth one side of his thick gray hair as a single wave.

"Step on him." Soileau smiled.

"It's faster and cleaner to pay him off," said a stout banker who'd previously stayed out of the conversation.

"Neither one will work," said Charles, and he told the story of Isaiah Clarke's wife, how the meteorologist had felt but could not grasp her slender fingers the moment she was sucked forever out into the Gulf of Mexico.

I realized that I was staring at Soileau's absent hand and shifted my gaze across the room to Mignonne sitting at a table of her friends. I watched the flits and flutters of her eyes and her bow-shaped, darkly painted mouth.

The men dissented. "No matter what his history," Hancock suggested, "every man wears a price tag. Sometimes it's just hidden. Often it's lower than you'd even imagine."

Charles shook his head. "Trust me. I've already had that avenue looked down. It's a dead end."

Even through the comfortable haze of the champagne as it diffused in my bloodstream for the first time in my life, this statement caught in my mind. I wondered how Charles had managed to have such a thing looked into. I wondered whom

Charles knew—what sort of men below him and what sort above.

Soileau bowed to Charles's analysis that Clarke could not be bribed. "Then we must neutralize him," he said. "Discredit him if possible—so much the better if with factual information."

Hancock nodded. "If the dirt won't stick, it will still serve us for now, but we need some time, so make it something difficult to out-and-out disprove. Innuendo, but damaging to his reputation as objective. A rumor about opium or something—I don't care for the details."

Soileau nodded. "Meanwhile, most important: we bombard the world with news releases saying exactly the opposite of anything that Isaiah Clarke says. And, for heaven's sake, it's time to lean on the governor with a little more weight. We cannot allow him to continue to stall until every penny from New York and Chicago catches the train back north."

When I awoke on Saturday, now seventeen years plus one day, I remembered only hazily the ride home from New Orleans. My headache was blunt, severe yet also transparent: I could almost see my way through it. I had driven, I thought, and I remembered a good-bye kiss from Mignonne's dark mouth, though perhaps that had been a dream brought on by staring too long at its curvy lines.

I was at once hungry and not. The coffee and bread smelled good, but the eggs didn't.

Such was my condition when Nanette arrived, breathing hard as though she had run the width of town, asking my mother if she could speak to me right away. In the new house, I observed, the distances were greater between rooms but sound carried more readily.

"Get your brother," I heard my mother say, sensing as women are said to do when the matters of life are more urgent than decorum.

Soon I was walking outside, wearing pants that reeked of cigar smoke and a hastily grabbed fresh shirt. I followed Nanette, who sought the shortest length of town between us and the woods that marked its circumference.

As soon as we penetrated a stand of loblolly, Nanette turned to me. "They took Henri away. My mother tried to hug him good-bye, and they shoved her away. My father tried to stop them, and one of them pulled a gun."

"What did Henri do?" Seeing the anguish on her face, I rephrased my question: "I mean, what do they think he did?"

"Nothing," said Nanette, her voice exasperated but low. "Only that he can stick pins in his fingers. Your father reported him for that."

My small world seemed suddenly as absurd as the world of the New Orleans clubs. The laws of physics, the bonds of cause and effect, seemed somehow broken or altered, and so nothing made sense. As though trapped in a strange dream or in one of those peculiar European stories Miss Fontenot had recommended, I understood nothing and worried that I never would again. My headache sat heavy on the balls of my eyes, and I remembered again that I might have kissed Mignonne, perhaps even at length. Focusing on Nanette's naturally pink mouth, I swiped my lips for traces of dark lipstick.

In a soft voice, Nanette said, "Louis, they've taken Henri to Carville. They say he has leprosy. They say my brother is a leper because he has no feeling in his fingertips. My mother tried to hug him before he left, and the men shoved her and told my father to hold her until they were gone or they'd take her, too. They said a doctor is going to come next week and test all of us."

She was not crying, nor did she appear as though she had been crying. The skin of her face looked thin, eerily translucent, and the purple shadows under her eyes were the deep shade of bruises emerging after a hit. But there was no puffiness or redness to those eyes, no suggestion of recent tears.

Hating myself even as I did it, I scanned the skin of her face, neck, arms, relieved to see no pock or mark other than the sole lovely beauty mark just above her collarbone.

What I wanted at that moment—and I told myself it was all I desired from my whole life—was to kiss that mark while Nanette held my head in her arms, telling me she loved me no matter what I did.

"I'm sorry," was all I could manage. "I'm sorry I wasn't here."

I listened to sheets of rain batter the metal roof as I watched Gaspar paint a canvas. Seven sketches—made on one of his rowing trips to the islands due south—lay side by side on the cabin floor to the left of where he stood. Gaspar turned only occasionally to gaze upon the leaded tangles of trees, painting mostly from memory or perhaps from personal vision.

At a glance, the seven sketches were nearly identical. Only as I studied them did I see how they differed. The shading suggested that some might have been made at different times of the day, but most varied only by the position of the artist, usually by his distance from what he was drawing.

"You can describe a tree from ordinary looking, but you will only understand it if it goes through you, if the image you make of it contains both it and you." As he spoke, Gaspar twirled his paintbrush between his long fingers, commanding it to blend red and green into black.

"Which version are you painting?" I asked, a little proud of having discovered the subtle differences in perspective among the seven sketches.

Gaspar shrugged. "Which one is the real one? Is a tree most itself in the morning or at dusk? When it's close enough to touch or farther away?"

From the cigar box of paints, I withdrew a black tube, pushing it toward him. I felt at first as though I were proffering a gift but then as though I were brandishing something sharp.

"Yes, I know," said Gaspar. "But that black, that black's not right for the pine here. It must be a color that isn't black itself but a black transmogrified from nonblack. You don't just see that; you know it."

I heard annoyance in his voice and knew that I should leave him alone to work. But I also felt my own impatience. I didn't want Gaspar's theories about color and angle of view but his advice about everything else, about the world that mattered to me, about my father and Nanette and the men in New Orleans and the rising river. I stared at the black that Gaspar had mixed and then at the canvas, pretending that my mind was engaged by his words, that I was considering them. When it seemed like enough time had passed, I waited a few seconds longer.

"Suppose you love someone and something bad has happened to them and you can't help them?" My words were low and awkward, almost a stutter.

"Hell, Louis. I don't know." Gaspar wiped his brush on the cloth hanging from his belt. He still sounded irritated but not quite so much. "You should ask someone who knows more about that kind of thing. If you haven't noticed, I live alone."

"Can I?" I asked.

Gaspar pointed with his brush in the direction of the smaller of the cabin's two rooms. All I wanted was to sit in that room, to see the whole world represented within its small, safe space.

The entire room was painted in mural to replicate the visual sensation of being outdoors across the year's seasons. Though the room was tight—not even twice my height in width or length—the walls seemed to peel away, falling outward to reveal, to each side, meadow in spring, marsh in summer, woods in autumn, and ocean in winter. Each habitat and season met peculiarly in the corners under a ceiling that depicted a seasonless sky about to rend with thunderstorms.

This world that Gaspar had fused was not without the force of destruction. But it was, above all else, beautiful. Yet because of its finite size, because it was fathomable, this world would not overpower me with either its violence or its beauty.

The security I felt was this: in this world, I could not make the wrong decision. In this world, I would not misstep and hurt someone.

After school a few days later, when I went to deliver the dentist's letter to Corinne Danger, I found the doctor's house locked and shuttered. I was staring at it from the street when Ann Washburn approached. Her neck blushed in red squares, and she fixed her eyes, shaded by the wide brim of her hat, on my face.

She spoke to me directly for the first time: "They've already gone, Louis. They barely even packed. They said they would send workmen to collect a list of belongings they wish to keep, said anybody could have the rest of their things."

"Running from the flood, do you think?" I asked, wondering if the whole of the town knew about Corinne Danger and the dentist.

She tilted her hat and walked back in the direction she'd come from. A few steps down the street, she said over her shoulder, "I don't know about them, but I guess a lot more folks will be clearing out ahead of what's coming."

On the way home, I decided that I would try to find out Corinne Danger's maiden name and obtain the address of her relatives in Lafayette so I could forward what I assumed to be a love letter. I reasoned with myself that I wouldn't be changing anything, merely passing along information. And I'd be fulfilling the wish made by a man in love.

The shallow footprints depressing the soil were proof that Emily at least had walked through the scent garden I'd planted for her. I looked for evidence that she had inhabited it in some fuller way, that she had pinched a lavender flower or thyme sprig or one of the now large leaves of lemon balm, perhaps putting it to her nose before rubbing it on her arms or neck. But in the rains the garden had grown too quickly lush to reveal such slight disturbance. Though it was sunny now for the first time in as many days as I could pass individually through my memory, the ground remained soggy.

In any account, Emily was not in her garden now, and I could not imagine where she might have gone alone, where she had been going alone. I rounded the back corner of the house, the line at which the half-painted house turned from the slate color my father had chosen at the paint store in Grenada to the dull, paler gray of the primer coat.

In the backyard, Luta was hanging linens on the clothesline she had strung at the sky's suggestion of a clear day. She held up her free hand and said, "I figured it won't seem like our house until we've lived in it a little. Baked some loaves and cakes, sunned some sheets, maybe had a family squabble."

Her tone was subdued but her laugh was as good-natured as

ever, and it comforted me to think that some things and people stay, over time, as they are.

"Let me help you," I offered. "You may have found the only day this spring for sunning sheets."

"Keep me company," she answered, removing one of the clothespins clipped like a fence down a flank of her light hair.

✦ ✦ ✦

In the late nineteenth century, half a dozen children infected with leprosy were removed from a pest-infested house in New Orleans and taken to the former sugar plantation at Indian Camp, a designation that eventually gave way to the name *Carville.* This may well have been an act of kindness.

Lepers entering the colony at Carville in the early decades of the twentieth century were encouraged, if not coerced, to change their names. It was thought that both the lepers and their families were better off parting ways for good. For everyone, it was easier in the long run. For the keepers of Carville, it was no doubt easier in the short term as well.

Decades later, when amateur genealogy overtook the country with the enthusiasm of any fad, in Louisiana even earnest researchers had great difficulty tracing relatives who had been interned in the Carville facility. Many a carefully drawn family tree had a stunted limb, a truncation bearing only the first name of an aunt or uncle or cousin who—though everyone had known where he or she had been taken—had disappeared as if forever into the mysterious word *Carville.*

✦ ✦ ✦

As I walked home from school, I fretted over Nanette's absence. She had returned to class a few days after Henri had been taken away but now was absent again. I worried that she was sick. I worried even more that, though she had shown no signs of lingering anger toward me, she had decided to avoid me. My stomach clenched when I imagined her realizing that I was the one who had told my father about Henri plunging needles into his fingertips. Helpless against the anonymous and armed authorities who had taken her brother, she would blame me. I had not meant to betray her, but events said that I had.

I recognized the singular sound of my grandfather's peg-legged gait before the old man caught up with me and was startled by its unusually rapid pace.

"Your father has been shot," he said when I slowed so he could overtake me. "He's lucid, but he took a bullet. He wants you to bring Rabbit to the company office and then come back here and ease the news to your mother and sisters."

Perhaps because I knew precisely what was expected of me, knew that any decisions would not be mine to make, I felt peculiarly calm. "Funes?" I asked.

My grandfather lifted the heavy slope of his shoulders in a shrug. "You'll have to ask your father about that," he said and accepted the short stack of my books before I trotted toward the Negro quarter.

Had it been only a few weeks earlier, I would have been fetching university-educated Dr. Danger. Instead, I was on my way to ask an untrained Negro veterinarian to treat my injured father—perhaps to save his life or to fail to. As I accelerated to the fastest run I could sustain for the distance, I vowed to destroy the dentist's letter to Corinne Danger.

Rabbit and I found my father sitting up in his small office in the back of the lumber-company building. Though the many papers were neatly stacked and the instruments ordered in rows, the surface of his cypress desk was covered.

"I can't work on you in here," Rabbit said.

Grimacing, my father shook his head. "I'm fine in this chair."

"This is about my work," Rabbit said. "We've got to move you so I can do my job." Finally he said, "I'm not asking you. You've got no choice."

I helped Rabbit carry my father to the front office. Rabbit supported his torso, and I held his legs under the knees. The room, which was used by Charles Segrist on his days in town, was large and less cluttered with evidence of occupation than my father's small office. I helped Rabbit stretch my father onto the wide, almost empty desk. It had a glossy surface and was made of cherry—one of the few common woods not harvested by the lumber company that owned Cypress. The air smelled like sanded raw pine, smelled like the walls.

My father had acquiesced to the move, but now he refused to let me go ask Ernest at the tunk for the whiskey Rabbit recommended. His face contorted, but he did not call out as the bullet was pulled from his shoulder with tongs and the ripped skin was trimmed with small scissors and sewn closed with a thick, coated thread. It struck me as odd that the thread was orange.

While Rabbit did this work, I looked past my father's head to the two frames hanging on the pine wall. One held a photograph, slightly faded, of a felled tree that was bigger than any I had ever seen. In trousers, suspenders, and a good hat, the man standing upon a trunk higher than most houses looked almost confident. But his shirttail hung out over the back of his pants and he held, ridiculously, a hand saw.

My father jerked his head toward the photograph and said through his teeth, "That's a California redwood. It's really something, isn't it? Maybe you'll see one someday."

"Yes, sir," I said, my eyes moving to the second frame. It held a map of Cypress Parish, its jigsaw-like pieces color-coded—red, turquoise, brown, pink, and white signifying the mix of woods each plot represented. I saw the pink where Rabbit's crew had been working and the white where Gaspar painted in his cabin.

"Should I tell Menard?" I asked after my father's breathing approached its usual rhythm.

"Why in heaven's name would you tell Menard about this?" He sounded invigorated by his disbelief at my obtuseness.

Embarrassed, I said something I should not have said in front of Rabbit: "Because he promised you protection." Anger mounting on top of—because of—my embarrassment, I added before I could stop myself, "And you paid him for it in kind."

My father stabbed me with a look. "It wasn't Funes, son. It was Jules Lançon."

I stared, my open mouth going dry.

My father answered my next question before I was able to

work up the saliva to spit it out: "Because I reported his boy for leprosy and the authorities took him off to Carville."

"What are you going to do?" I managed to say.

"What do you think I'm going to do with a man who shot me?"

For a moment I thought he planned to kill Nanette's father. My throat tightened, and I touched the desk to keep my balance.

Then he added, "I can't say I wouldn't have done the same that he did, but I am the law around here and have to act it. I'm sure he expects to be arrested. He may even turn himself in."

Nanette's breathing grew heavy as though her lungs were collapsing and enlarging with unnamed weight. I closed the door to Gaspar's shed and moved with Nanette through its muted light to the room whose walls were painted like the seasons.

In the eerie light, Gaspar's stylized images looked more natural than photographs. The trees and animals seemed more real than the walls on which they had been painted. I watched as Nanette made hard quarter turns, jerking her head like an inexperienced ballerina to take in wall after wall after wall after wall, and then looking at each of the four again. She blinked several times and made sounds more amphibian than human language.

I understood the meaning of this slowly—fully only when she sailed open the folded sheet she had carried with her, covering the dirty rug that was the room's only furnishing with the crisp pale-green linen, barely a shade darker than the dress she had worn the day we'd lost our virginity to each other. I noticed the slight difference in hue, I thought, because we were in Gaspar's cabin, because he had taught me to think about color and because he would have noticed such a detail.

Unlike the first time we were together, when I'd fumbled with her strange girl's clothing to gain rudimentary access to her skin and then to all of her, this time Nanette removed everything she wore, even sliding the breadth of white ribbon from her hair and removing the ankle socks that kept her new sandals from blistering her feet.

I assume that I undressed myself, but I am not sure of it. I do not remember how I came to lie on my back, all of my youth and sadness and confusion and guilt prone before Nanette Lançon's beauty. Yet I remember exactly how it felt when she knelt beside me and then over me. I remember the precise curl of her soft hair spilling over her white shoulders and the heaviness of her breasts and the smooth curves of her hips and stomach. I remember the abandon with which she took me, because it was something I did not encounter again for many years. I remember the intense effort I expended to hold on, to make everything last forever, and the way she screamed softly, calling at the end, as she faced the wall representing meadow in spring, "Butterflies, butterflies, butterflies."

Afterward I lay still on the sheet, just becoming aware of the friction burns on several of my vertebrae. I knew that Nanette had given herself to me fully—her real self and not just her body this time—and I wondered why.

She walked around the room, looking again at the murals while I watched her naked body. Her shyness seemed utterly gone, and it came to me then: a knowledge that I could not articulate but was fast. Sometimes I wonder whether I merely transposed what I learned later onto that moment—one of memory's many tricks—but I believe that I did know, just then, at that precise moment. What I knew was that Nanette would make love to me only one more time. It would be another payment, half now and half on delivery, for getting her father out of jail. I knew that the next time she would use her will to hold herself within the boundary of ecstasy that she had crossed this time, that she would break her hips to make me finish before she did. I knew then, or so I remember it, that Nanette would give herself completely to me only once, and that this solitary time was already part of a past, already growing distant.

As Nanette walked around the room, I already knew, too, that as an older man I would think back on what I could have done or said at that moment that would have made things different for us. But a young man does not see his future as something he can change, because he does not see his future as already fixed. You cannot alter what part of you believes is wide open.

Nanette leaned over to flip through a stack of the canvases propped against the summer wall, pulling them one by one toward her so their tops rested on her bare, pale thighs. The sight of her hip, stretched taut by her position, caused an ache in my chest that made me look away.

I heard her stop her rhythmic flipping as she lingered long on a single painting.

"Louis," she said, sounding nearly astonished, "this one is Emily."

✦ ✦ ✦

The finest anatomy available prior to modern times was Galen's. Galen, a physician in Rome, wrote his anatomy based on his studies of the bodies of gladiators. He examined their wounds as he treated them, taking detailed notes in an elegant if slightly cramped hand. The inaccuracy of his drawings suggests that he did not dissect the bodies of the fully defeated. And so his work remained strictly observational. He could chronicle how bodies were made but not, for the most part, how they worked and certainly not why. Such explanations were—wisely, it was generally deemed—left to philosophers and poets.

✦ ✦ ✦

✦ ✦ ✦

Everyone knew that a break on one side would spare entirely those on the other. As the river rose and rumors spread of multiple crests, each at unheard-of and almost unthinkable measures, people eyed the bank across the river.

When it was clear that the river cut more deeply against that far side, if a curve in the riverbed forced the current harder against the opposing levee, or if that levee was known to have been built to lower, earlier standards—in these cases people looked across the river with pity, with sympathy. Some even made plans to help later, if necessary, to bring food and supplies after the fact, to work charitably and side by side with their unfortunate neighbors.

But when such was not the case, when their own side's levee was the more suspect, their own position on the river the more precarious, then people's feelings toward the towns they looked across at were something else altogether. Sometimes these people felt an envy bordering on hatred.

Whatever the case, one's own levee had to be guarded in all circumstances and at all cost. Armed men, by foot and by boat, patrolled stretches of levee from the upper tip of the Yazoo-Mississippi Delta to those places south of south, those places where the Gulf itself made all levees irrelevant, a luxury of more northerly places where land and water are distinct.

Any man seen approaching a levee was warned away with

buckshot or other ammunition. Anyone seen buying or carrying dynamite was followed with vigilance and risked never being seen again.

✦ ✦ ✦

Olivier Menard received Charles and me on the ground floor of his closed casino. Because of its smell, the spacious room seemed smaller than it was. The smell held aftermath: spilled liquor and beer, cigarettes and cigars already smoked, and, I imagined, grave error and the despair of lost money and perhaps hope.

A mulatto woman made her way methodically around the green felt tables, combing them with a wide piece of stiff paper or cardboard. Though she wore absolutely no makeup and was approaching old age, she was indisputably beautiful. I attributed her beauty to the structure of her facial bones and the smooth egg shape of her head when viewed from behind or in profile. She held her back and neck straight, lending a startling elegance to the low work of her hands.

Menard served us cold bottles of beer on a small wooden table near the casino's closed back exit. Charles pulled his bottle from his mouth in surprise, nodding in approval at the large gulp of liquid still held in the expanded pockets of his cheeks.

Though Menard did not appear to watch Charles, he said, "The casino doesn't keep it on the menu, but I have my own beer sent from a village outside Prague."

I had seen or heard the name of that city a few times, but I could not have pointed to it on a map of the world.

Charles raised his bottle to toast, but Menard concentrated on pouring his beer into one of the tall, chilled glasses he had himself carried across the room on a tray.

"Here's to the Czechs," Charles said, almost merrily, clinking his bottle against my still-untouched one.

"Proust," said Menard.

I imitated the tall man's movements, lifting and tilting the frosted glass, pouring the beer at an angle into the side of the glass, controlling the foam as it grew in depth, sipping slowly. But then—without realizing I was about to—I licked away the mustache of froth left behind in a manner that made me feel childish.

Menard met my eyes and smiled. "Are you enjoying the story of the *Beagle*'s voyage?"

I nodded and started to comment that Darwin's descriptions always focused on smaller life, on the natural world, at the expense of the humans around him. "For stretches, it seems that he is sailing alone, that no one is even helping with the boat," I began. "As though he were sailing a one-man pirogue," I was about to add.

Charles interrupted. "I did not realize that my two friends were already acquainted with each other."

Menard spread his smile, again at me. "We have not much of a history—only a short one—but we have established our own rapport, Louis and I."

Charles lifted his sand-colored eyebrows at me, possibly amused but perhaps annoyed as well. Then he shook out his hair, which was as far from a haircut as I had ever seen it. "Never mind. To the business at hand."

Menard rose when the door opened. "Our other friend is arriving now."

I set down my raised glass without sipping from it, paralyzed by indecision as Orlando Funes strode the breadth of the casino floor. As the undecided most often do, I did nothing.

Funes stood beside the table and did not sit until Menard indicated with a clear gesture that he should take the empty chair, which I had seen but failed to note as significant, failed to realize was waiting for someone. Menard then called over the mulatto woman and directed her to bring in another beer and glass.

"We all know what they want to do, and that it is in all cases against our interests." Charles stopped to make eye contact with each of us. "What we need to discuss are two items. How to fight it," Charles said.

"How to dissuade them," Menard corrected.

"Yes, how to dissuade them from dynamiting the levee. And also we must consider a fallback position, to consider what we are willing to do if they cannot be dissuaded, how much we are willing to give and, most important, for what in return."

"Out of the question." Funes's first words were pronounced in heavily accented English, and he did not smile.

"We may be unable to prevent them from blowing one of our levees," Charles said. "We must get the most we can out of them in that event."

"We all know you sleep in two beds," Funes said, his voice soft. "One full of the fleas of expensive dogs."

The conversation paused while Funes took the bottle of beer but refused the glass from the woman, who retreated back to her work grooming the game tables.

"You are right," Menard said to Funes, pressing a glance to

forestall any response from Charles. "But so is he. We have a great deal of power down here because no one really cares much about down here. We are south of south, neither land nor water. We are nowhere. All our power here is nothing away from here. We have little pull—maybe none at all—with the city Bourbons. In the end, it is likely that they will do as they wish. Our best option is to convince them that dynamiting the levees of Cypress Parish is not what they wish to do. Perhaps they will arrive at the view that it will cost more to blow up our levees than to leave them be."

Funes's cheekbones twitched, tightening the pocked skin of his already narrow face into a hatchet. Without hurry, the man who'd wanted to kill my father and was stopped only at cost looked at each of us.

Charles said, "Perhaps they will draw the conclusion that it is less expensive to dynamite another levee, someone else's levee."

But I knew that all the levees downriver from New Orleans protected our parish.

Funes nodded and seemed to chew the inside of his cheeks. "I have decided to agree. But *non* to what you call fallback position. Our fallback is guns and dynamite of our own. That will show them what their best interests are. In the trapper quarrels, I learned there is never shame to die as a man. But with these men, with their pretty daughters and pretty things, they do not want to die."

He turned to me. "We are not soft people, you and I."

I felt something like pride in the coarse and callused hands I had so recently planned to soften. And I was ashamed to have been ashamed of them.

My father sat in his armchair, which he had angled toward the picture window of the new house's living room so that he could see some distance up the street. I stood at the window, for a moment looking in the direction my father looked, trying to see what he saw, albeit from a different angle.

And then I honored my unspoken pact with Nanette: I pleaded with my father to release Jules Lançon, at first with no visible effect.

"I know what is behind this, who is behind it. You may not have thought about this, but consider that I know what it's like to think you're in love with a pretty girl. But you never, not ever, put anything ahead of your family. Lançon had his motives, I'll grant you that. But he tried to kill me. He tried to kill your father. You don't ask anything of me on his account."

"But he won't try it again." I treaded for words before I comprehended what I had to do. "Besides, you need him. He owns a business in Cypress Parish. You need Menard, and you need Mr. Lançon. You need all the French and Isleños, every one of them. You need every Catholic in the parish."

My father held himself straight, his lips sealed. The sling that held his right arm to immobilize the shoulder kept the arm unnaturally high but limp. For the first time in my life, I felt that I had a thing my father wanted. I knew something that he didn't.

I let him wait, but not long enough to find out how long he would have waited.

"They've been meeting in New Orleans. They want to dynamite our levees to save their city money. Mr. Segrist says they won't listen to a bunch of crackers, but they might listen to Catholics with property. If not, it doesn't matter about jail because we'll all be flooded out. We'll all be underwater. You'll kill him if you don't move him."

✦ ✦ ✦

Life at Carville improved after the facility, together with its grounds, was purchased by the federal government from the state of Louisiana. Inmates became residents, albeit permanent and usually involuntary ones. Even those few who were granted permission to leave after a miraculous year of clean tests rarely did. Most did not have the means to go, and they knew that they would not be welcome elsewhere. Others simply preferred the company of those who did not cringe at the word *leper,* those who could look them in the eye and feel no revulsion.

Goto baths and chaulmoogra oil showed promise as treatments, and conviviality characterized Carville society as residents nourished a little theater, built a Quonset hut to serve as a locker room near their golf course, and organized Mardi Gras krewes. As might be expected, Carnival balls and other events involving the wearing of masks were among the most popular entertainments at Carville.

✦ ✦ ✦

Unlike my cautious first trip, I felt at ease with the drive into Grenada to pick up Olivier Menard. In my ease and with my new sense of purpose, with the contentment that derives from being part of big things, I felt almost important as the mile markers and shaving-cream signs clicked past.

"Smart company," Charles said, nodding in approval at the signs. "Wave of the future, that kind of advertising. Soon everyone will have everything he needs. That's when men after more money will have to get clever. If your artist friend is ever down on his luck, that might be just the business for him."

"Gaspar's not down on his luck," I said.

"I suppose not. Not unless you consider living alone without two dimes to rub together down on your luck." Charles spoke like himself, but his smile was at bay. Lack of sleep or else worry or perhaps just a stack of drunken days lined his forehead and pulled like gravity at his mouth.

As we approached Grenada, he spoke only once more. He said, "Louis, I must extract a promise from you. You must promise to tell nothing of what you hear today and tonight. To no one. That means not to your girl and not even to your father."

He was silent after this, and I imagined that I had avoided producing the promise. But as we walked Menard back to the long car, Charles slowed me by the elbow and said, "I am sorry to ask this of you, young Louis, but I do require your word on that matter. If it helps, you should be flattered that I consider you a man of such honor that I require only your pledge." Still holding my elbow, he turned to face me. "Your word is enough, but I must have it."

"All right," I whispered. "You have it."

He nodded and dropped his grip.

"Are we picking up Orlando Funes?" I asked when we were back on the road. "Or meeting up with him?"

Menard looked over his shoulder at Charles, who said, "Neither. He is no longer part of this. He's chosen another approach."

After a polite silence in which I heard only the sounds of the car, the crunch of shells, the shrill purr of cicadas, Menard spoke to Charles. "No mention, not for hours, of fallback," he said. "For hours we do not mention reparations. We do not give, as you like to say, a whiff of it early. We argue hard. We argue with great force. We argue as though we are stubborn of necessity, as though we must win the argument and will argue until we do. Only then—only then!—do we even listen to the word *reparations,* do we even hear it."

I followed their conversation as closely as I could under the wind and the preoccupation of driving with no illumination save the diffuse powdery light of the headlights.

When Charles, after a pause long enough to notice, did not respond, Menard continued, "The less likely they think we are to accept anything at all, the more they will offer." He looked across the seat at me and then made eye contact with Charles through the rearview mirror. "The higher they will start, and the higher we will finish."

Even though I had paid attention, concentrating on the words spoken, it took me several minutes to understand what had been said, what was being done. In those minutes, I wondered where Funes was, what my family was doing, whether

Gaspar was in Cypress or on the islands. It was then that I guessed the extent of the fine that had been levied against me—the price of the promise I had already made.

In the towns of Cypress Parish, as in towns throughout the many other river-run portions of the country, residents varied in their flood preparations. The details of their readiness fluctuated by whether they believed in destiny or random outcome, by age and by experience, by which of their possessions were important to their ways of life, and—often—by simple degree of industriousness. The lazy do not necessarily brim with newfound energy in times of emergency, though, of course, there are always exceptions to any general principle.

Responses ranged from moving valuables to high shelves and the boarding of windows—as if hurricane preparations were applicable to any impending catastrophe—to full-scale evacuation or even detailed plans for permanent relocation.

In our brand-new home, my hardworking mother and sister carefully wrapped and packed our most valuable belongings. Those most precious to my mother—the family Bible, the few photographs, and those letters she deemed important for sentimental or other reasons—were mailed to a cousin too distantly related to descend upon in the flesh. She was chosen to receive our most precious material possessions solely because she was the relative who, by virtue of marriage to a salesman in Birmingham, resided farthest from rising water. My mother added to the package, at almost the last minute, a pair of infant shoes worn in turn by me, Luta, and Emily, though not, because my father had purchased new ones, by Pal. She also dropped in her wedding locket and a diary of sketches that I had not known she kept.

Our other valuables were shipped as freight, under my father's selection and direction and following the guidance of Charles Segrist, to one of the lumber company's offices in the Florida panhandle.

My mother and Luta moved the other pieces of our household to the attic, when possible, and to the second floor as next-best choice. Due to his wounded shoulder—where the muscle had been torn under the skin—my father was unable to carry great weights up the stairs. Even then, I understood that this was a humiliation.

When home, I did all that I could to help. At other times, the women had to get by with what help they could draw from Pal. This is one of the things about my life of which I am ashamed.

✦ ✦ ✦

On the night of April 25, 1927, not quite two dozen of the most respected men in New Orleans—including the board chairmen of all the largest banks and their most trusted lawyer—met in a private room of the Hibernia Club with representatives of the business interests of Cypress Parish. The bankers and the lawyer who accompanied and often talked for them held no public office, elected or appointed. And the representatives of Cypress Parish had not been chosen by the people of that parish or even by its chamber of commerce.

Everyone who spoke that night, and speaking that night was a form of action, was self-appointed. These were men who—it was said and they themselves would certainly say—took matters into their own hands.

✦ ✦ ✦

Charles hinted at reparations far earlier than Menard did and certainly much sooner than Menard had recommended. Only half an hour deep into the April-night meeting, it was clear that the dynamiting of a levee in Cypress Parish was a foregone conclusion.

Numbers and procedures were now the subject of debate, with the one-armed lawyer and Charles arguing furiously over the size of reparation accounts, the question of whether to permit or forbid the filing of partial damage claims, and the relative monetary weights of property losses and lost income.

This discussion had proceeded at length when Menard interjected for the first time in the details: "What about loss of life?"

Hancock, who Charles had told me was the wealthiest man in the room and was rumored by those in the know to have been last year's Comus, raised his palm. "There will be no loss of life. Word will be spread early and far, and evacuation will be conducted with the best of organization. We will rely on only the latest and best of human engineering."

"There will certainly be loss of life. Always, there is loss of life," Menard pressed. "Someone will not be found and thus will not be told. Some others will refuse to leave their homes no matter what."

Soileau answered, "We cannot be responsible for those too obtuse to leave."

Menard looked solely at Charles and asked, "Nor for those who cannot be found?"

"If they cannot be found," said Soileau, with an expression approximating a smile, "then they will not be missed."

Again Hancock lifted his open palm, pushed against the air as though it were solid. "Mr. Soileau is overly zealous in his love for our wonderful city, and so I must state a correction. If there is any loss of life, and we will do everything possible, including pray, that none will occur, then any family members who come forward will be compensated more fully than can be expected. I give my word as a man of honor—and I will ask the rest of the fine men in this room to do so as well—that the good, that the heroic people of Cypress Parish will suffer no uncompensated loss."

I did not have a seat at this table but sat as rigid as I could in a straight-backed chair against the wall, just behind Charles's right shoulder. I listened as the men swatted the final remaining point of contention: the constitution of the board that would process claims and arbitrate any disputes.

Soileau was adamant that the representatives of New Orleans dominate. "It's our money to protect against fraud," he said.

A compromise, which seemed to favor the city only slightly, was reached when Hancock again offered his promise of good intentions as a man of honor and solicited the same from the others present.

It was this, it was Hancock's word, that seemed to sway Menard. And it was Hancock who phoned the governor and elicited his promise to sign what was being drafted. The governor would sign the night's work, provided, he insisted, that four lawyers could be found who would pronounce unambiguous legal opinions that he had the proper authority to approve the dynamiting and that he would incur no personal liability should he do so.

"We already have one lawyer," Hancock stated evenly. "We will get you the other three by dawn."

"Covering his *derrière,*" Charles said. "And a large one it is."

Menard snorted and then smiled at me as the discussion broke into small and more personal conversations and many of the bankers retreated from the room. "I suppose it's just a matter of when. You make sure your family leaves with everything that's important, Louis. Don't forget to take *The Voyage of the Beagle* with you. If nothing else, it suggests that a journey can lead to discovery, that knowledge can come from discomfort."

Not one of the other men still present—not even Charles—turned his head to look at me.

✦ ✦ ✦

In the 1940s, the medical director at Carville, in collaboration with the staff of research laboratories in Hawaii and elsewhere, discovered that sulfone drugs readily cured the disease long believed to be, at the least, incurable and, quite possibly, a direct and deserved curse from an unmerciful God.

Residents campaigned—largely through the organ of their nationally distributed magazine *The Star*—to rename their affliction Hansen's Disease and their home the Gillis W. Long Hansen's Disease Treatment Center. This effort had a great deal of success in the medical community, and even in Louisiana, people were more or less willing to call leprosy Hansen's Disease at least some of the time. But the local population never could adjust itself to calling the old Indian Camp plantation anything other than *Carville.*

When the patients' softball team, the Point Clair Indians, won the 1951 River League baseball championship, one local paper carried this lead line: "Carville Lepers Take First Place."

✦ ✦ ✦

After the meeting in which the bankers formalized their intention to dynamite a levee in Cypress Parish, Charles stayed on in New Orleans, giving me leave to use his car after returning Menard to Grenada.

"It is a terrible thing that will happen," Menard said when I dropped him off to make my solitary way home.

The distance from Grenada to Cypress now seemed brief to me, though it was long enough for night to become morning.

At home, we ate breakfast quietly. I watched Pal dissolve most of a biscuit in a glass of milk. Emily held hers in her hands, smiling at its warmth. Luta was the only member of the family who ate with real appetite. After the meal, while my mother and sisters tidied the kitchen, I followed my father into the living room. He took his usual armchair and stared through the front window.

"While we've got two cars here," I said, "maybe we can drive some more of our things away."

"Which things? To where? You think that man's fancy car is going to hold the new stove? You think it's going to carry our new house to high-and-dry land?"

I looked down at my feet, which were squeezed into Charles's spare pair of brown wingtips, and then to my father. Seated in the soft chair and sunk into his still-slung arm, he looked smaller than I had ever seen him.

"No, sir. I just figured we'd have to do the best we can."

He nodded, his gaze still directed through the picture window at the hard-driving rain. "We will, but it's not going to be good enough." Then he added, "We're going to do our best for others, too. Town will mostly know by now, but we'd better get word full around the Negro quarter and to the folks in the woods. Don't forget that painter you're friendly with, Gaspar, and get the word to those two families that live across Tiny Bayou. You know the French word for *flood?*"

I nodded and whispered, *"Le deluge, inundation."*

Gaspar was not in town and not, as I'd hoped, in his cabin. I wanted to tell him what was happening, of course, but even more for him to tell me what to do. I knew that he had probably rowed out to paint on the islands, where he sometimes spent a night and sometimes stayed much longer. He would not get word of the dynamiting there, where there were no human inhabitants. Unless he happened to be on his way back already, not only the shed itself but everything it contained would be swept the full distance to oblivion by rushing water. I remembered what my mother had said about backwater flooding: there's nothing *just* about backwater flooding if you live on backwater.

I entered the cabin, walking by Gaspar's current work to the smaller room, where I tried to memorize the murals of the four seasons. Only a few people had seen them—Gaspar, I, Nanette—and I would be the last person to see them. My chest thrummed, my throat tightened, and I was very close to crying. I couldn't save them, I told myself, but I could rescue some canvases. I flipped through the stacks leaning against the wall, remembering the position of Nanette's limbs the day she'd made the same motions. I passed by birds and trees, insects and a seascape, before I came across a painting of a person. This time, not preoccupied and spent, I looked with care at the painting of my sister.

Emily filled most of the left side and middle of the canvas. Though her image was off center, leaving room for enormous, craggy blackbirds flying violently from a point behind her, the view of her was straight on, not angled. It cut her off at the knees, making her seem even larger.

She stood in a thin white shift, which clung as though wet to her body, showing the slope under her rib cage, the twinned snakes of muscular stomach, the knob of her left shoulder. Her other shoulder was eclipsed by her gleaming hair, loosened, its ends webbed but with loose strands whipping around her neck as wildly as the birds—both frightened and frightening—in their crazed flight.

Child of nature, I thought. Then my eyes cast on the shape of her small breasts, the almost obscene red of her parted lips, the flare of her nostrils, and I thought, *Not child, something else.*

Though I could have carried several canvases, I took only one small painting—one of trees, one of three visions Gaspar had distilled from the seven similar but unique sketches. The square painting was not—not in my opinion and not in Gaspar's—his best work. It was a study of studies, the work of just a few days. It was, I thought, an object worthy of rescue. It was also a painting I had been a part of; I knew that was some of my motivation.

While I might have next made every effort to find Gaspar or

to seek help in moving his paintings to higher ground, or at the least to an attic where they might have stood a chance, I did not.

Later I would tell myself that I had not gone straight back to town to recruit extra hands because I needed to get to the families across Tiny Bayou as quickly as possible. It was important—in case they had not yet heard the terrible news—to give them the longest possible time during which to absorb the reality of *le deluge,* to pack up or shore up their possessions, and to leave.

After looking a final time at the painting of Emily, I faced it to the wall. Where I had sensed tragedy that no one would ever see the painted walls of the four seasons, I felt something like satisfaction in thinking that I was the only person, other than the man who had painted it, Nanette, and perhaps Emily herself, who would ever see the painting of my sister.

Several nights before the levee was to be dynamited, twenty armed men visited the fine homes of Hancock and several other men who had signed the pledge to compensate Cypress Parish for its sacrifice. Among them were men who hated each other, including former enemies in the trapper wars, including bootleggers and their foes, including men who had taken shots at one another. Among them were Orlando Funes and Jules Lançon and—his hunting rifle propped against his left shoulder, its butt cupped oddly in his left palm—William Proby.

The posse's exact purpose was not clear, even to its members, but these men left holding fast to the belief that they had made a point. If nothing more, they had at least interrupted more than one fine dinner. They had shown their faces to those who would soon owe them. They had shown themselves to be men.

Before they dispersed, each to attend to his own important business, these men slapped each other's backs. They shored up in each other the belief that their action had ensured that promises made would be promises kept.

✦ ✦ ✦

In the days that followed, residents of Cypress Parish traveled north and east to the homes of relatives, if they could. If for the usual reasons of economy and family feud they could not flee to such relatives—or if, as was often the situation, all their relatives lived in places that already were or soon would be underwater—they moved themselves and what else they could into the International Trade Exchange warehouse in New Orleans. The fifth floor had been designated for white flood refugees, the sixth floor for black.

Some residents, no doubt more of them white than black, were assisted by trucks sent by the National Guard or by the several New Orleans retailers influenced by charitable leanings, a mind for public relations, or quite probably both.

In New Orleans, members of wealthy families as well as others who could call in their good connections sought permits to view the dynamiting. Those lucky enough to obtain them looked forward to the final day of April, when—with packed lunches and cold beverages—they would head for Cypress Parish in cars, yachts, and hot-air balloons. Not one person whose permanent address was located inside the parish was awarded a permit to view the destruction of their levee. Naturally, few belonging to this category applied in the first place.

Meanwhile, airplanes, hired on the city's behalf by Monroe Soileau, circled low over the parish. Their pilots scanned for remaining residents. But their primary task was to take the photographs that would protect New Orleans against exaggerated claims of loss by those who might take advantage of personal calamity to replace a small house with a large one or a failing enterprise with a profitable one.

✦ ✦ ✦

I unloaded the boxes and suitcases I had earlier packed into Charles's car with an eye to the limits of geometry. Sometimes I used the warehouse freight lift, but it was often less trying to climb the five flights of stairs with the lighter boxes. With the heaviest things, I had to wait in line for the lift. This line was not so much long as it was clumped thick with entire families and their myriad belongings. Though I was certain I had laid eyes on everyone who lived in the town of Cypress, I didn't know most of the people. And so I wondered just how much land and how many towns were predicted to flood.

On my final trip up, I had difficulty getting out of the lift with a heavy trunk. Only with trouble did I make my way around two black families whose destination was the sixth floor. Once out, I dragged the chest to the place I had staked out for my family—an area of floor I'd chosen because it was not too far from a large window and so not as dark as the corners of the room appeared to be. I thought it was the place my mother and Luta would have chosen, given the options available.

It was also within sight of Betsy and Ann Washburn. I was grateful for the familiarity of their faces and relieved by the idea that we could look out for each other. People seemed anxious, and I sensed that anxiety and desperate behavior are few steps removed.

Charles invited me in and tossed the car keys I'd just handed him into a wooden bowl on a side table. His face showed fatigue, and he looked several years older than he had the day he'd shown up at our house in time for dessert, asking my father if I could be his driver. His reddish hair still had its spring, bouncing when he sat down hard in his chair, but his affect was flat. He spoke and moved more slowly than usual.

When he noticed me looking toward the empty kitchen and then to the hall, Charles said, "I am quite alone today, Louis. It's good that you have come because I am horribly lonely and may well be horribly lonely for the rest of my wretched life." He sipped what looked to be the melted ice of a drink nearly gone. "Time for another. At least I have someone to join me this time."

"I'm sorry," I said, uncomfortable at seeing him like this and also at my inability to think of something wise or at least clever to say. "Where is Mignonne?"

He rose and disappeared behind me, and from the kitchen I heard the sounds of drinks being mixed.

"I can't stay," I said, albeit not forcefully enough for Charles to hear if he chose not to.

He handed me a highball glass with a strong, unfamiliar smell. "Bourbon," he said, smiling ruefully. "Time for you to taste a grown man's drink."

I sipped it twice, uncertainly both times, before setting it on one of the coasters on Charles's coffee table.

"Mignonne has gone, Louis. I knew the day had to come, indeed that it was coming. It's time for me to start my adult life."

I waited.

"But I didn't know it would hurt her so badly." He collapsed, head falling into his hands, and convulsed. "Or me. I didn't know I would miss her so much," he spat out as he cried with great force, breaking down.

"I'm sorry." I picked up the drink again and tried a larger sip, which burned my palate and throat.

He continued to cry into his hands, and I sipped a bit more from the bitter drink. It seemed indecent to leave him, so I waited longer before saying, again quietly, "I cannot stay long. I should try to get back to Cypress to drive my family out."

I had hoped, albeit shallowly, that Charles would offer me a ride back to Cypress. Now that hope dried completely.

He seemed to hear what I had said in delay but then straightened quickly. "Nonsense. I need you here. Besides, all roads lead out today. There's no way to get you back."

I wanted to believe him. I wanted to believe him because the drink hitting my blood was making me want to stay and have more and because I did not really want to walk and hitch my way back to a place that everyone with sense was streaming from. I wanted to believe him because I did not want to spend the night in that warehouse of strangers. Most of all, I wanted to believe him so I could do what most people want: to do as I wished while telling myself it was best for others.

"I need company," Charles said. "I am not in a good state."

And that was enough. I drank the final long pull of the highball and nodded.

"You're a fine friend, Louis. What would I do without you? I'll go make a call to the big store and get word to your family not to wait for you. And I'll pick us up some more ice while I'm at it. You get yourself cleaned up. You look like you've been doing manual labor, heaven forbid."

"Tell them, when they get to the warehouse, to look for our things near the Washburn women. Tell them I will find them there."

I listened to the door close behind Charles and for the sound of his steps descending the stairs. Only then did I picture my parents and siblings, Nanette, Gaspar. Only then did I admit to myself that I was doing something wrong.

The following morning, I drove Charles to the yacht club, where we were to board a sailing boat and make our way to the site by water. Charles was dressed in his cream-colored suit and a new green tie. Despite the previous long evening of drink in his closed apartment, he looked sharp. His eyes were again bright, and the suggestion of premature aging had passed from his face.

I knew that, in contrast to Charles, I looked barely presentable. I had slept poorly and in the morning had felt almost sick from the whiskey, the lack of food, and the stifling air of the apartment whose windows we had failed to open at nightfall. I had cleaned up, but my hair was unruly. That the sleeves of the jacket borrowed from Charles were inches too short made me look more ridiculous. I tried again to beg off, certain now that I should meet my family as soon as possible.

"Nonsense. I need you to help me get through this."

On the deck of the boat, he introduced me to the woman whose family owned it. Elizabeth Turner wore her blond hair in a loose bun at the nape of her neck, a blue-and-white dress like the crisp sails of her yacht, and pale makeup that barely showed. She was mostly pretty, though her jawline was squared by a slight underbite, and this gave her a look of permanent dissatisfaction.

She kissed Charles's temple when she handed him an iced tea garnished with mint. He received the kiss with a smile, though he did not lean into the touch and, in fact, remained completely straight and, except for the smile, still.

"Thank goodness we decided against driving," she said to me as well as to Charles. "The traffic is sure to be dreadful. It seems that everyone and his cousin want to watch this thing. It's quite the gala event."

✦ ✦ ✦

Several days before the scheduled dynamiting, a molasses tanker rammed the levee south of New Orleans. This occurred in Cypress Parish, remarkably close to the place selected for dynamiting. The break was small; some of the river did flow through, but to little effect.

By an equally astonishing coincidence, the tanker was owned by the family of a friend of the banker Hancock, a friend who claimed connections to the governor's office and a man who had heard firsthand the reports that the governor was still not fully convinced that the dynamiting was necessary. The governor had commented to the city engineers that their predictions of a flooded New Orleans would come to pass only if the upriver levees held. And that was, at the least, an uncertain likelihood.

Despite the legal opinions assuring him that he would not be held personally liable for the destruction of life or property in Cypress Parish, the governor had been stalling. "I am ready to sign when it is clear that it is necessary," he told those who asked. "But I will not sign until such time."

✦ ✦ ✦

Charles helped Elizabeth lift the anchor, and she laughed as they dropped it into the water with a splash. The boat we were on was one of hundreds bobbing smartly white on the brown, swollen river. As if perversely, the sky was a broad blue, like a clean and unfurled sail, unpunctuated save for the shining sun.

I could hear pieces of conversation from other yachts, so close were they. Some of the talk was of the dynamiting: the way the river would feel like a carnival ride as it descended after the crevasse opened, estimations of which portions of the sacrificed parish would flood, talk of how long it would take for the water to fall in New Orleans. But most of the talk was of other things. The women's voices spoke of parties and summer travel and hats and food. The men spoke of sports and politics and, above all, of the business of money.

"Where is Menard watching?" I asked while Elizabeth was below deck, preparing our lunch and, at Charles's insistence, pouring something more serious than iced tea.

"Louis, Menard agreed to the plan because he recognized he had no choice. He is certainly not the sort of man to watch men destroy what he's made for himself in this world."

"You're watching." I spoke caustically even as I realized that my anger was misdirected, that I was mad at myself for being in the wrong place, for having let that happen.

"True, my boy, but Menard's situation is different from mine. His interests are all in Cypress Parish, and unlike me, he's got family and history there. My trees will still be standing after the flood subsides. And anyway, I've always said that my true interests lie in New Orleans. Maybe with Elizabeth at my side, they'll let me into the Louisiana Club, and maybe they won't. But I have been useful to them, and they know it."

"Mignonne was useful to you," I said, tasting bile.

He laughed, even good-naturedly. "You're a smart young man, Louis, I'll give you that. And you're right that maybe the best I can hope for is to be paid to go away, knowing that I'll be missed."

Though divers positioned several rounds of explosives just as the spectators were finishing their lunches, they succeeded only in making the levee cough enough to open a six-foot-wide ditch. The water that moved through it was more stream than flood. It was clear that much more would be needed to release the force of the river across Cypress Parish: several tons of dynamite before the long day was over.

More than half the crowd went home well fed but with their appetite for excitement unsated.

Charles rebuffed first Elizabeth's hint that we turn back for the city and then her suggestion that we do so. After a while, she asked directly, mentioning her sunburned nose and tendency to freckle.

"I'll be under your orders soon enough," he said sharply. "But today I am determined to see what we have come to see. I may even owe it to young Louis here."

I scanned her face for anger, but she seemed more satisfied than annoyed by his position.

"All right. So it is," she said. "I'll put on a hat and open another bottle of champagne."

We were not the only boat on the river when the levee finally blasted open, but no other boat remained close to us when we fell—falling is how it seemed to me—as though dropped like a stone from the sky.

After I steadied myself, I looked up to see the water, rising in a wall so high I could not fathom its top, crash through the fresh crevasse. I had never imagined the water would be so great. My home would not flood but would be swept away as though it had never been made.

I still held my glass, though in the boat's fall all of my champagne had spilled across the deck.

✦ ✦ ✦

The day following the flooding of Cypress Parish, the levees of several tributaries to the lower Mississippi failed and blew out with no human intervention. Instead of pouring into the already tall river, their waters rolled across the Atchafalaya Basin and almost harmlessly out into the Gulf of Mexico. The flooding of Cypress Parish was thus proved, in fewer than twenty-four hours, to have been unnecessary to save the city of New Orleans.

By the time this was known, every acre of the parish was submerged. The final wall of water and its resulting currents destroyed the great majority of homes and killed almost every land animal there. Nearly every home that still stood would be ruined after sitting in months of water.

✦ ✦ ✦

PART THREE

CREVASSE

✦ ✦ ✦

In 1543, Garcilaso de la Vega, reporting secondhand on de Soto's Mississippi River expedition, described a natural flood: "It was a beautiful thing to look upon the sea that had been fields."

Not quite four hundred years later, a dozen men took turns flying small planes across Cypress Parish, radioing the whereabouts of people stranded on rooftops to the hundreds of volunteers waiting in all manner of boat save yacht.

The pilot of one of the planes was among the casualties resulting from the dynamiting of the levee between Grenada and Cypress, though his widow's appeal for compensation would be denied by those representing the city of New Orleans. Those representatives argued with success that the man might well have been flying and indeed might even have crashed on that same day, albeit probably somewhere else. It was an act of God, one lawyer asserted, and there was little that the banks of men could do when faced with the acts of God. "Sometimes, it is simply a man's time to go," he concluded.

Those who witnessed the crash—flood refugees waiting to be rescued from mound or rooftop or tree branch—said it was a graceful fall. The plane dipped one of its wings, the right one, and swooped toward the rushing water. "Like a bird from the future," said one woman.

It is possible, though we can never know, that the pilot's last impression of the sea that had been land was that it was beautiful.

✦ ✦ ✦

hough I had left behind the jacket, I still wore Charles's clothes. I climbed the many flights of stairs first quickly and then, nearing my destination, slowly. I was frantic at first and then pressed upon by dread. I forced myself up the final length of staircase, taking several steps at a time.

I was out of breath when I opened the door to the fifth floor and so was surprised by the quiet living within. People had spread themselves about atop bedrolls and blankets. They were sleeping or reading or sewing or talking softly or just sitting and looking straight ahead.

Across the floor—across hundreds of people who behaved in familiar patterns yet were unknown to me as individuals—I saw Betsy Washburn standing to stretch as though she had just awakened. I picked my way toward that section of the enormous room, trying to keep my shoes from touching anyone's makeshift bed, still waiting to catch sight of my family.

When I found them, my mother embraced me tightly, weeping and kissing the side of my head. I leaned into her, wishing I was a child, as Luta and Emily embraced me from behind. We stood huddled like that for a long time.

My father did not interrupt, and it was somewhat later that he spoke to me at all. When he did speak, it was before the window I had chosen for us. There was no true privacy in this place of so many people, but we could stand facing the window, looking out, so that we did not see the crowded room behind us. The checkerboard of smudged glass panes overlooked a street, gray in the steady drizzle, lined by a row of warehouses. Beyond that was another row. And beyond that was the river, its might hidden by its levee. No one moved about the street, and the huge doors of each warehouse were chained closed.

"We waited for you, waited until almost the last minute. You will never know how much your mother and sisters worried about you. They worried that you were on your way or that you were lost and would not get out in time."

"Daddy had to drive," Pal said from behind us. "With his shoulder all slung up, he had to drive."

"Powell, don't eavesdrop. You go ask your mother if she needs your help with anything. Right now." My father's voice was harsh yet weak in volume.

"Charles said he would call with a message that you should get out quick and I'd meet you here."

"Well, I don't know about that. All I know is that you should have been with your family, one way or another."

I stared at the locked-up warehouses, loosened my neck muscles by tilting my head to each shoulder, and let a few moments pass—the only answer I had. "What about the Lançons?" I asked at last. "Have you seen them?"

"That's what you've got to say to me?" my father said slowly, seeming to me to withhold maliciously whatever he knew about Nanette.

"They would have done it without me, you know. They were going to blow the levee no matter what any of us did," I said.

I heard Pal sidle close again and told him to get the hell away. He scrambled to where my mother sat brushing Emily's dark hair and looked away.

"Of course they would have done it without you, and you should have let them." My father spoke in a hiss.

Long-smoldering confusion and anger ignited, and I flung words at him like fists. I recalled the union man whose face my father had beaten bloody, the mere pennies given to people the lumber company had swindled out of their timber rights. In an order that was not chronological and indeed had no logic, I named every failing I had ever associated with my father. Then, nearly shaking with the potency of the realization, I reminded him that he was the one who had stuck me on Charles, told me to learn what I could from him, told me to let him use me like a servant boy in order to learn his world and his ways.

"That's what you wanted for me. And perhaps," I almost

shouted, feeling the powerful crescendo of finale, "perhaps you forget that I was there when you struck your sordid little pact with Olivier Menard. I heard what you did, what you offered him like a coward."

I waited to be struck by fist or by open hand, but my father simply stepped back and took a seat on one of the plain wooden folding chairs that were now our only furniture. He lowered himself slowly at first but then dropped, almost a fall, at the end, as though his knees rather than his shoulder were injured. He nodded without looking at me, shook his head, nodded again.

"There was not much choice in my life." Now he found my eyes and looked directly at me, though still he spoke softly. "All my decisions were about *take it* and *leave it*. I'd like to have people think otherwise—I'd like to have you think otherwise—but I'm an uneducated backwater nothing. I knew it, though. At least I knew it, so that every time I had the chance to stay behind or move ahead, I chose progress. Even when it went against my own nature, even when it cost me a layer of your mother's respect, I always chose the *take it* half of the *take it or leave it*. And one of the reasons I did it was so that my son would have the luxury of exercising a finer moral judgment than I could ever afford." He made an effort to straighten his posture against the weight of the injured shoulder. "It seems that you have learned the wrong things from me. Maybe that's my fault; maybe it's yours."

I had always thought of shame as a hot thing. In the novels I had read, the characters were always burning with shame. But on that day, as the air drew the dampness from my skin, leaving behind a chill despite the warmth of the maturing day, I learned that shame is quiet and cold. I shivered with it as my father continued.

"You've accomplished a rare feat, son. You compromised your integrity without getting ahead. I guess I could make a joke about selling yourself downriver, but I don't even want to think about water." He laughed, perhaps at me.

I dropped my head, and he made a strange grunt, a sound that suggested that not merely the conversation but something larger was over.

"To answer your question: the Lançons got away from the water all right. But Jules Lançon said he won't let the river get him again, said he's only got it left in him to start over one more time."

"Are they here?"

"On a train to California, where it hardly rains at all."

That night I slept spooned between my sisters under a quilt my mother had stitched from scrap fabric. Exhausted from lack of sleep and the flood of emotion, I slept well despite my shame, despite my longing to see Nanette if only for a final kiss, despite the increasingly foul odor of so many people in such close quarters.

Over the next days, I learned more about the last dry hours of Cypress Parish. One day Pal burst into tears, and Luta told me he was crying because our father had shot Terrebone.

Animals were not welcome in the refugee stations, particularly if they were not vital to a family's livelihood. The occasional pig or chicken was tolerated on the sixth floor, but it had been decided that no animals would be permitted on the white floor. My father said he couldn't leave Terrebone to drown or starve and so dispatched him with a quick bullet to the head.

"That's why Rabbit's probably dead, you know." Luta said in a voice made eerily calm by too much drama. "He decided to stay," she said, "to try and save his animals, try to ride out the water with them." She looked up quick, as with a new idea. "Think he might have made it?"

For a moment I hoped with Luta that Rabbit had secured himself and his animals on his tar-paper-covered metal roof. Or perhaps he had cushioned them in rowboats or somehow lashed together a raft.

But already I knew better, and I shook my head. "It's too much water, more water than you could ever see all of."

I pictured Rabbit's yard as it had been the afternoon he'd set Terrebone's broken legs: Rabbit standing, the animals eating or sleeping in their pens, the snakes still plump and tangled around a tilted branch. I saw all of the creatures as they were, merely submerged as if in a huge aquarium. The light in the yard was dappled not by fluttering leaves but by the movements and distortions of water. In this vision, Rabbit's large palms are open toward his animals. He is laughing, but I cannot hear the sound through the water.

I looked for Gaspar Anderson but couldn't find him at the refugee warehouse. I didn't unwrap the towel that protected the painting I'd taken from the shed, but I checked on the canvas several times a day, if only to assure myself that I still had it. I told myself that he must have heard about the dynamiting, that he had probably rowed his paintings to safety.

But even if Gaspar had saved his canvases, I knew that he could not have rescued the murals that were the walls of his shed. I understood that those trees and birds and the butterflies whose name Nanette had called out in passion were lost forever to water. Still, I told himself that they could be repainted and tried to imagine what Gaspar might have to say about that idea.

The city of New Orleans successfully prohibited the filing of claims for partial or estimated losses. Cypress Parish residents unable to return to their homes, or the plots of land where their homes had formerly stood, were not allowed to file interim property claims. Each family could file only one claim, and that claim would be considered final and comprehensive. Some—out of money and so not able to wait—filed only for lost income, forsaking entirely their right to be compensated for all that had been washed away.

This was the situation of Betsy and Ann Washburn, who took their small check and moved away to Mobile after working out a side deal with my father. He offered them about one-quarter the value for their boardinghouse and the deed to the big store. Ann, in a rare show of strength against her more extroverted sister, argued that this was the best deal they could hope for. After all, my father had promised to send the money even if neither structure still existed. He was known to be a man of his word, if nothing else. He was getting either a sweet deal or the worst deal of all.

Jules Lançon, with my father's help, eventually filed his claim from a distance. Many of the lost dollars he had counted on were ruled out on various technicalities. For what remained, he was paid nineteen cents on the dollar. Monroe Soileau himself approved the final figure.

Orlando Funes received nothing at all, perhaps because more than one banker remembered the night his dinner had been rudely interrupted by armed men from Cypress Parish. The lawyers for the city—under Soileau's direction and overlooking the fact that muskrats are in fact farmed more than hunted—declared the rodents property of the state, a natural resource owned by no individual. As the rest of his income had long stemmed from illegal activities, Funes was unable to file for his nontrapping losses at all.

Only Charles Segrist and his lumber-company associates—none of whom lived in the state of Louisiana—received full compensation. Olivier Menard, despite the illegal nature of much of his income, fared better than most. There are obvious advantages to sitting at the tables where decisions are made. If nothing else, those with power had looked Menard in the eye when they'd made their promises.

In my natural history, I described several of the more unpleasant species to inhabit bayou and marsh, including moccasins and swarming fire ants. The flood lifted thousands of venomous water snakes and millions of stinging insects from their bayou homes. They spread across the parish in thick clumps. Traveling the many currents, they ruled the surface of the submerged world for weeks, frightening even those people in high-walled boats. As weeks gave way to months, the reign of small monsters weakened, though they menaced for a good long while.

✦ ✦ ✦

In 1998, officials announced that the Gillis W. Long Hansen's Disease Treatment Center in Carville, Louisiana, would close its programs and its gates. It was noted that while leprosy still crops up in Louisiana and pieces of Texas—almost always the result of eating the meat of infected armadillos—the disease is contagious only through prolonged domestic contact and is now readily cured. It was argued that any moneys devoted to the disease were best spent on physician education, on reminding doctors to keep the malady in mind when diagnosing patients, particularly from those cultural groups most likely to eat armadillo.

Some of the money was spent on an educational brochure, which was mailed out to doctors across the southern half of the state. Inside was an illustrated joke. The riddle read, "How do you know you're at a Cajun zoo? There's a recipe in front of every cage." After several doctors claiming Louisiana French ancestry complained—some on the dubious grounds that poor blacks were more likely than Cajuns to eat armadillos—the brochure was redesigned without the cartoon.

The remaining residents of Carville, most but not all of them elderly, were told to choose between placement in another long-term-care facility or independent living with a modest stipend and free medical care for life.

Many protested. Some had lived at Carville since early childhood and had married and buried spouses there. Some were sentimental. Others, particularly those with the most extreme facial deformities, were motivated by a clear understanding of how the rest of the world would see them. They did not want to leave a place where people, even those with whom they did not get on well, could look at them without wincing. Eventually the government consented to allow the Sisters of Charity, an order whose history is not separable from the care of lepers, to run the colony.

Today the last few Carville lepers live out their months or years in the stately brick original buildings and the characterless dormitories built in the postwar decades. Most have made their life's work a museum of Carville, where the sulfone drugs were developed, the drugs that eventually cured their incurable disease but could not undo the damage already done. Some research the identities of the original Carville children. Others write up reports—and, in at least one case, a doctoral dissertation—on various aspects of life in Carville across its many decades. And so they live out their lives behind the hurricane fence, a fence whose gate now remains unlocked during the day but, at the behest of those living within, is tightly secured at night.

A number of residents, however, were pleased to leave. Among those accepting the stipend to strike out on their own was an elderly but notably spry resident who used the name Girard Arbeaux—a man who had been incarcerated at Carville as a teenager after a town official reported that he could stick needles into his fingers without pain.

Girard Arbeaux found a small apartment on Magazine Street

in the city he had never been allowed to visit as a young man, when he had badly wanted to.

Accustomed to routine but by nature a lover of variety, he took his breakfast at the same diner each morning until he had exhausted every possible combination on the menu, at which point he changed morning haunts. Careful observers noticed not only the odd thick patches on his face but also that he ate exclusively with his left hand, never raising his right arm to table height and thus never into view—not even to angle a knife, lift his cup, or signal for the check.

He never attempted to contact his remaining kin, nor they him. While a regular patron of his third breakfast establishment, he died one night in his sleep. Unlike his upstairs neighbor—who had not been missed until his smell rotted the hallway—Girard Arbeaux was discovered by his landlord before his body was chewed away by insects and humidity. Once embalmed, that body was entombed in the charity mausoleum behind a Catholic church that Girard Arbeaux had never once attended. The story was written up by an aspiring freelance journalist who frequented one of Arbeaux's favorite diners.

Girard Arbeaux might well have preferred his burial place to the groomed rows of the Carville cemetery, which had been moved to the pecan grove in 1921 to allow building expansions over the previous burial grounds.

One of the new buildings, one that stands today, is the Union Chapel erected in 1924. A blend of Mission revival and the neo-Gothic, the masonry-and-wood building is admired for its leaded amber windows and ornate woodwork. Though it has been mentioned as a possible location for the Museum of the History of Carville, some residents have objected on the grounds that the chapel is still used for worship.

✦ ✦ ✦

✦ ✦ ✦

The flood of 1927 contributed directly to the election of Huey Long over the incumbent governor, the man who had finally—albeit reluctantly—approved the dynamiting of the levee south of New Orleans. It was later agreed that this move had been unnecessary to save the city. Indeed, the city leaders themselves quickly launched an impressive and thorough public relations campaign declaring that the Crescent City had never, not for a moment, been in any danger of flood and in fact was highly unlikely ever to flood.

Many in Cypress Parish did not vote in the election that inaugurated the Long era because their homes and businesses—if standing—remained accessible only by boat. But in the coming years, Long could depend on Cypress Parish, despite the high prevalence of Catholics living there, to help him defeat the Bourbons of New Orleans. It was his sole rock-solid base of support in the southern portion of the state.

In one election, Olivier Menard promised Long by phone that of the tens of thousands of Cypress's votes, only two would go to the Bourbon slate of candidates. When the Long-supported slate won the parish unanimously—not a single citizen voting in dissent—Long asked Menard what had happened to the two men who had been set to oppose him. He was told, by a droll Menard, that they had been persuaded to change their minds.

Though Jim Crow was not so severe in southern Louisiana

as it was in some other parts of the south, racial discrimination and other gnarled manifestations of power and its imbalances prevented many in Cypress from ever casting a ballot. Yet it can be said with little doubt that the pro-Long votes reflected the will of an entire populace.

✦ ✦ ✦

Due in no small part to the help of my father—who imposed upon the consciences of Charles Segrist and Olivier Menard—and thanks to a patience derived from the assumption that they would receive nothing, the Lançon family was paid some compensation by the city of New Orleans.

Several years ahead of the hundred thousand who would struggle their way to southern California fleeing too little water rather than too much, Jules Lançon did well for himself. He bought cheap land—land that could be irrigated but would never flood. He planted oranges and a few olive trees and began to build his final enterprise, this one enduring.

I obtained this information from my father not too long before he died, old and of natural causes. After years of my own inquiries, which I admit were casual, I had mentioned my curiosity about the fate of the Lançon family. To my surprise, he told me that the man who had once shot him had corresponded with him off and on for a fair number of years. But all my father knew of Nanette was that she had taken some lessons at an acting school and had once been paid to pose for a billboard advertising a new soft drink.

Much later in life, indeed as I was entering old age, I found myself at a garage sale. I was, that day, accompanying my wife as part of her ongoing search to replace broken pieces from the rock-crystal wine glasses her grandmother had bequeathed to her.

Leaning against a suburban driveway fence, on sale for a quarter, was a war-bond poster. A woman jumped from an invisible diving board, wearing a diaphanous gown that revealed as much as it veiled the full curves of her body. Her hands were thrown in the air and her back was arched. It was, I had no doubt from the moment I saw it, Nanette Lançon with her curly dark hair, rich lips, heavy breasts, and air of being in a better place—or at least a different place—than those around her.

I wondered what had led her to pose for such a picture, thinking about the day she had walked naked around Gaspar's cabin, all her self-consciousness hidden. Perhaps, I told myself, she'd posed out of patriotism, or financial need, or sheer longing for a lover sent across one ocean or the other to fight in the war.

✦ ✦ ✦

After disaster, many people distinguish themselves by helping not only their families but their neighbors. In 1992, after Hurricane Andrew—which killed dozens of people and proved to be the most expensive natural disaster in history to that date—the populations of several small towns in southern Louisiana refused to apply for federal emergency relief funds.

"We help our own," one man said in a thick accent, when asked by the national media. Others shrugged before the cameras and said that the time required to file for compensation would not be worth what would come of it. Some said the claims would never be paid anyway. One woman, who would not be filmed and who refused to give her name to journalists, said, "It's better if they don't know who you are or where they can find you."

Taking matters into their own hands, residents donated materials to the effort and generated work schedules based on need. Homes were quickly rebuilt, businesses put back in order. It is, apparently, easier to help others when disaster is natural and one is no longer in harm's way.

✦ ✦ ✦

The flood and then the Great Depression reversed my family's fortunes. Yet—having procured the remarkably sturdy boardinghouse and general store at flood prices—we fared better than most.

I was sent to the state university. There I lived frugally as I took the courses that could have led me to medical school, as my father had planned and for several years believed would happen, but that instead carried me into a life of science. From the university, I made my own way, taking my pick of several good graduate schools and learning to speak more like people on the radio.

Given my decision to study fluid mechanics, I worked in relative obscurity during the war years. But later my work brought me prestige and offers of well-funded facilities at fine institutions. I believe my father was proud of me when he died.

Though I have always enjoyed seeing my siblings, I haven't had much in common with them and did not often travel far from my laboratory save to visit my wife's family in Maine or to conferences—most often held in California or Scandinavia or London or Toronto but sometimes in China and, once, in Santiago, where the buildings looked as I expected them to and the street performers had beautiful voices.

Luta eventually earned a college degree, a few courses at a time as money permitted, and became a schoolteacher. She married a kind and well-read carpenter for love, and they lived near Cypress in a small house with a yard full of dogs and flowers.

When I visited, we'd force ourselves over to Powell's house

for Sunday dinner, though Luta generally washed dishes during coffee and dessert so we could make an early getaway.

By the time Powell finished secondary school, no one still called him Pal. He fulfilled my father's dreams of a doctor son and took a specialty in internal medicine. He married a small, intelligent, and ambitious woman—one energetic and practical enough to help him run offices in both Grenada and Cypress and to rear three children in one of the area's large new interdenominational churches.

Emily never came to Cypress Parish, not even when I visited, though the door to her New Orleans flat was, she said, always open. Luta, but not Powell, visited her regularly.

Though Gaspar Anderson had not been in love with her as anything other than a subject, Emily had been in love with him. Or, rather, as he painted her, she had fallen in love with the smell of his paint. Eventually she fell in love with the wonderful and horrible smells of New Orleans as well. The city, she told me over the phone once, was close-feeling and warm, a small city she could make her way around by nose and by touch.

After a few years of painting in near squalor, Emily gained a cult and then a wider following. Her large canvases, painted directly by hand and finger with thick smears of vivid color, hung in galleries of improving reputation and, eventually, in the art museums of New Orleans, Houston, Dallas, Charleston, Little Rock, and St. Petersburg, Florida.

She never married, though at the age of thirty-five she did take a somewhat younger lover and helper. He freed her from such material obligations as cooking and bookkeeping so she could work with fewer interruptions and even greater concentration.

The presence of this man in her home may well have been the reason that our churchgoing younger brother failed to visit. Of course, Powell had always had an aversion to the eccentric.

In 2003, one of the Carville nuns died in a car accident that was reported in local but not regional papers. Another Sister of Charity was injured—broken ribs, bruises, whiplash—in the crash and shortly thereafter transferred to Corpus Christi, Texas. In an interview, she stated her intention of returning to Carville in the coming year. The sooner the better, she said. "Louisiana isn't the kind of place you leave and stay gone from," she explained.

A lot of people say this kind of thing about my native state, but for me it has never been true.

During one of my rare trips south, one of my last, I excused myself from the hospitality of my brother's family, rented a car, and drove the two-lane highway that wends along the Gulf of Mexico, trespassing on pieces of Mississippi and Alabama on its way to the Florida panhandle.

I stopped in a small town just inside the Mississippi border, a town visited only, but frequently, for its antique shops and a couple of good restaurants, including one regionally famous for its chocolate *pots de crème.* Near the center square, I found the small museum dedicated to the works of Gulf Coast artist Gaspar Anderson.

I paid the nominal admission charge to the Acadian-style house and read the posted literature. Central to the museum's vision of Anderson was the interpretation of the flood of 1927 as tragic. In the opinion of the museum's curator, a man not without impressive credentials, the paintings lost to the flood would have enhanced the painter's reputation and perhaps brought him to national attention—not, it was emphasized, that the artist had ever sought such prominence. On the contrary, Gaspar's final years had been comfortably obscure. He had married late and happily and had been fortunate enough to work into old age.

Just inside the exhibit area was a sketch, made based on an interview with the artist, of a fully painted room representing change over time. The original room had been lost to the great flood. Unable to bear more than a glance, I made my way along the walls of paintings. Much of Gaspar's early work, which had been given by the young artist to various friends and acquaintances, had been found and assembled here.

Between that and his later, markedly more stylized paintings, hung only three works. Two of these had been sold by the near-penniless Anderson to a gallery in New Orleans just before the flood. The third was the small study of trees that I had carried from the shed shortly before the dynamiting of the levee. The latter had been identified by a colleague of the curator in a second-hand store in the suburb of Metarie, a place best known to the rest of the country as the source of David Duke's first electoral victory.

As I gazed at the small, dark rectangle, I remembered the series from which it had come and could not recall how or why I had chosen this one. That I might have saved more than one from the group—or saved the portrait of Emily—was too awful to think about. The peculiar wash of emotion I felt can be described only as guilt.

Among Gaspar Anderson's later works were few human portraits. Most of the paintings were distorted and angular interpretations of birds, insects, and small mammals, including a painting of a muskrat group grotesquely yet almost humorously presented.

It was a single painting that preoccupied me for the twenty or so minutes I remained in the small place of homage. It was titled, simply, *Deluge* and appeared on first glance to portray, albeit vividly, only swirling floodwaters.

As I stared at it, I could see splintered wood churned in powerful, circular currents. A few minutes later, I found also white rectangles smeared with jewel-colored tones. I was watching the floodwaters from the exploded levee destroy Gaspar's shed. I was seeing the flood submerge forever its muraled wallboards and the paintings housed therein. It was a painting of loss.

While I knew that it could be a work of imagination, inspired by so powerful an event as betrayal and the demolition of one's life work, I didn't believe it. I had witnessed the artist's methods and heard him theorize about angle and vision. Gaspar had shaped my own methods of observation, my own understanding of the relationship between the inductive and the deductive, between the particular and the general, and between objects associated by time or space. I'd learned as much from him as from anyone.

I studied the lines of perspective and relative sizes and contemplated the side-view angles of the trees poking through water until I found the artist's eyes. Gaspar, on his boat, perhaps knowingly or perhaps returning unaware from the coast, had watched the flood tear apart his shed and suck his work into the brown whirlpools.

I continued to stare at the saturated canvas, watching it grow smaller as I backed to the door.

The year following the flood of 1927, engineers, some of them upstarts, in addition to others who had been educated the hard way, set about designing levees and dams to hem in the Mississippi once and for all. This time they neither overlooked nor ruled out the benefits of outlets and spillways, though a decision was made to keep the Mississippi where it was, no matter how badly the river wanted to jump for and conjoin with the Atchafalaya.

Flooding was corralled with unprecedented success in all but a few places, places left to the foolish or unusually greedy and thus of no great general concern for several decades. Later people forgot about the big floods and began to move in larger numbers into the floodplain—not out of stupidity or avarice but from necessity. It was after the severe flooding of 1993 that insurance costs caught the public eye.

The price of the magnificent if imperfect control achieved after the 1927 flood was the withholding of sediment—over time, a significant amount of it—from its destination in the deltaic plane. Naturally, the construction of navigation canals, the work of oil and gas exploration, and the nature-made destructiveness of hurricanes performed their work as well.

Between 1932 and the century's end, nineteen hundred square miles of Louisiana's marsh washed away. Much of what had been lost was once home to black bear and American alligator and wintering ground for many a migratory songbird, including those species fond of the seeds of the ancient bald cypress. Also gone are many of the state's lucrative shrimp and oyster nurseries. Experts state that, should the year 2050 actually arrive, one-third of the state's shoreline will be gone. Politicians in Baton Rouge and sometimes even Washington discuss this issue from time to time.

But coastal erosion is not a routine subject of conversation in Cypress Parish, where life is as hard as ever for the poor, most of whom have continued to pull what living they can from the strange mix of land and water that is their home. It is them that I think of now, on the eve of a new destruction that will be made worse by the loss of what has washed away, trying to remember what it felt like to be the boy that I was.

Among my small pile of possessions in the warehouse, I found the letter intended for Corinne Danger—crumpled in anger and never mailed but never destroyed. It struck me that it represented random fate. Had her affair not been exposed, Corinne Danger would not have moved to Lafayette ahead of the flood, and the dentist would not have gone wherever it was that he went. Had I mailed the letter, together with one of my own telling her how she could trace her lover, things might have been different—or not—for both of them. But we never get to see that other roll of the dice, that other arrangement of matter, and so we can deceive ourselves into thinking that things happen for a reason, that they turn out as they are meant to.

Back in 1927, several hundred miles north of Cypress Parish, near Greenville in the Yazoo-Mississippi Delta, white homeless residents were evacuated from the levee. Blacks who had made their way to the levee top—or who had been brought there by boat in missions that could be described either as rescue or as conscription—were organized by overseers into work crews and paid in meager food rations.

In one such place, on one day, a steamer sent to evacuate stranded people was ordered to turn back empty save for a few dozen white women and children. Labor was already in such short supply that plantation owners had schemed to lure poor immigrants to the delta even before the flood. And the gun-holding overseers were under strict orders to prevent any workers from escaping. The doctor on board, claiming the agency of the Red Cross as well as that of the federal government, challenged them to shoot him.

When they decided that they could not shoot the doctor and finally stepped aside, about two hundred black men, women, and children made their way, in twos and threes, up the gangplank. Perhaps to the surprise of the overseers, a good number of these evacuees later returned to sharecrop the land that steamed when the water, at long last, went away.

But, as might be expected, all did not return to the fertile soil owned by others. A young girl was sent to live with her uncle and his bride in Memphis, presumably to a better life, though the details of that life—the ways in which it proved itself better or worse than a sharecropper's plight—I do not know.

One young man, not yet out of his teens, made his way north to Chicago. There, under the tutelage of an elderly musician, he became one of the Windy City's finest drummers. He grew wealthier than many, dated a series of beautiful women, then threw himself from a skyscraper after failing to mend a heart broken by a married woman—reported to be quite plain in appearance—who in the end had refused to leave her husband.

Certainly, from that group saved by the brave physician from the waves that licked the levee top and from the National Guard members who ruled it with force and through fear, there are many such stories of fortunes changed. Some lots were no doubt vastly improved, while another few, subject to the same capricious fate, were greatly reduced.

I think about those people again tonight. Disaster ruptures everyday life, and it disrupts fate. Before the flood, I had one life and set of concerns. More than anything else now, more even than the secrets of chaotic motion, I would like to know what my life would have been had it not been disrupted. I wonder how my young love affair with Nanette would have ended, how I would have negotiated the pull of the city, what I would have said to Gaspar Anderson had I stumbled upon him painting my thinly dressed sister. I am denied these scenes; one of the things you lose when you make a choice, or have it made for you, is the knowledge of what would have happened had things been different.

Because of the crevasse in my life story, I am denied even closure. I never saw Nanette again, and I never saw Gaspar except through his painting. On many nights, late, I imagine parting scenes as though watching a grainy film. I imagine myself running through the Negro quarter to convince Rabbit to evacuate, holding Nanette's hand as she tearfully waits for the train that will carry her all the way across the country, delivering to Gaspar the painting I saved and trying to explain why I did not save the portrait of Emily. But these are fictions; I cannot know how those encounters might have unreeled. I live with only imagined alternatives to the choices I made, and the choices made for me by chance. Although I have put together everything I know, still I cannot say what happened.

Acknowledgments

Cypress Parish is not merely a fictional place but a geographic impossibility. Nevertheless, some of this novel's events are based on historical and familial record. I am deeply indebted to, and drew liberally from, two books: *Rising Tide: The Great Mississippi Flood of 1927 and How It Changed America,* by John M. Barry, and the unpublished, untitled memoirs of my maternal grandfather, Robert Elliott May Sr. I also used information published (both in print and on the web) by the Livingston Parish Historical Society, the Historical Society of Vermillion Parish, the Gillis W. Long Hansen's Disease Treatment Center, and the Public Broadcasting System. But I alone am responsible for the (sometimes intentional) historical inaccuracies contained in this book, and none of the fictional characters is based directly on any real person, living or dead.

I am grateful to David Bajo, Esme Claire Bajo, Meredith Blackwell, Will Blackwell, Martha Powell, Tim Parrish, Joe Queenan, Howard Norman, Yvette Dede, and several colleagues for various forms of support and encouragement in the writing of this book. Thanks to Fred Ramey for the exquisite editing and to everyone at Unbridled Books for bringing this work to print. Portions first appeared as "Seeing Water" in *Seed* and "After Carville" in *Witness,* for which I am indebted.

A Note About the Type

This book was set in Dante MT, a typeface designed by Giovanni Mardersteig (1892–1977). This Monotype version was released in 1957 and is a modern interpretation of the Aldine type used for Pietro Cardinal Bembo's treatise *De Aetna* (1495).